THE NEWCASTLE FORGOTTEN FANTASY LIBRARY
VOLUME V

ALADORE

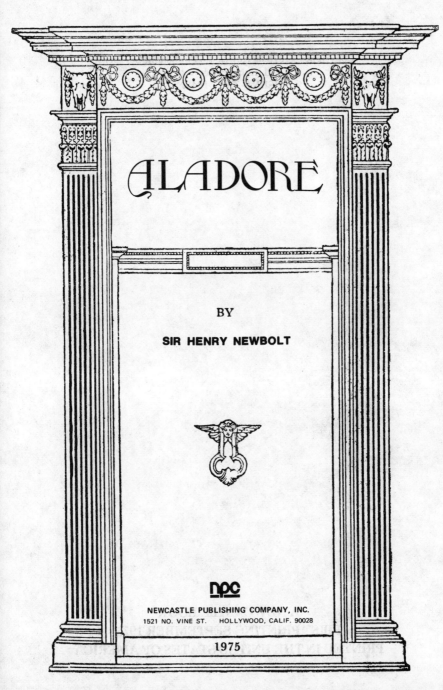

ALADORE

BY

SIR HENRY NEWBOLT

npc

NEWCASTLE PUBLISHING COMPANY, INC.
1521 NO. VINE ST.   HOLLYWOOD, CALIF. 90028

1975

A NEWCASTLE BOOK
FIRST PRINTING SEPTEMBER 1975
PRINTED IN THE UNITED STATES OF AMERICA

CONTENTS.

v

Contents

Contents

Contents

Contents

ix

Contents

ILLUSTRATIONS.

———

Illustrations

In every land thy feet may tread
Time like a veil is round thy head :
Only the land thou seekst with me
Never hath been nor yet shall be.

It is not far, it is not near,
Name it hath none that earth can hear :
But there thy soul shall build again
Memories long destroyed of men,
And joy thereby shall like a river
Wander from deep to deep for ever.

—Dream-market.

ALADORE.

—◆—

CHAPTER I.

OF THE HALL OF SULNEY AND HOW
SIR YWAIN LEFT IT.

SIR YWAIN [1] sat in the Hall of Sulney and did justice upon wrong-doers. And one man had gathered sticks where he ought not, and this was for the twentieth time; and another had snared a rabbit of his lord's, and this was for the fortieth time; and another had beaten his wife, and she him, and this was for the hundredth time: so that Sir Ywain was weary of the sight of them. Moreover, his steward stood beside him, and put him in remem-

[1] Ywain = Ewain or Ewan.

A   I

brance of all the misery that had else been
forgotten.

And in the midst of his judging there was
brought into the hall a child that had been
found in the road, a boy of seven years as it
seemed: and he was dressed in fine hunting
green, but not after the fashion of that day or
country. Also when they spoke to him he
answered becomingly, but in a speech that
no one could understand.

So Sir Ywain had him set by the table at
his own side, and now and again as he judged
those wrong-doers, he cast a look upon the
child. And always the child looked back at
him with bright eyes, and even when there
was no looking between them, he listened to
what was being said, and smiled as though
that which was weariness to others was to
him something new and joyful. But as the
hour passed, Sir Ywain felt his mind slacken
more and more, and whenever he saw the
boy smiling, his own heart became heavier
and heavier between his shoulders, and his

life and the life of his people seemed like a
high-road, dusty and endless, that might never
be left without trespassing. And though he
would not break off from his judging, yet he
groaned over the offenders instead of rebuking
them ; and when he should have punished,
he dismissed them upon their promise, so that
his steward was mortified, and the guilty
could not believe their ears.

Then when all was said and done the hall
was cleared, and Sir Ywain was left alone
with the boy.

But the steward, looking slyly back through
the hinges of the door, saw that his lord and
the child were speaking together ; and he
perceived that they understood one another
well enough, though how this should have
come about he was not able to guess, having
himself heard the boy answering to all questions in none but an outlandish tongue.

Then he saw Sir Ywain rise up, and suddenly he was aware that his lord was calling
for him loudly and with a hearty voice, as

he would call for him long since, when they were at the wars together. And when he went in, Sir Ywain bade him summon all the household.

Now when the household were come into the hall they stood at a little distance from the dais, in the order of their service, and Sir Ywain stood above them in front of the high table. And beside him was the boy, and before him was his own brother, who was now an esquire grown, with hawk on wrist.

Then Sir Ywain bade his brother kneel down, and there he made him knight, taking his sword from him and laying it on his shoulder, and afterwards belting it again round his body. And he took the keys from his own girdle and the gold spurs from his own feet, and said aloud: I call you all to witness that as I have done off my knighthood and the Honour of Sulney, and given them to this my brother Sir Turquin, so also by these tokens do I deliver unto him

the quiet possession of my house and goods
and the seisin of all my lands, to hold unto
him and his heirs for ever, by the service
due and accustomed for the same. And
henceforth I go free.

Then his brother, who was both glad and
sorry, and moreover was still in doubt how
this might end, stood holding the keys and
the spurs, and looking at him without a
word. And he looked also at the child, and
he saw that for all the difference in their
years, the eyes of Sir Ywain had become
like the boy's eyes: and as he looked his
heart became heavy, and for a moment he
envied his brother and feared for himself.
But in his fear he moved his hands, and
the keys clanked and the spurs clinked
together, and his heart leaped up again for
oy of his possessions.

And all this Ywain saw as it were a
great way off, and he smiled, and forgot
it again instantly. And the boy took his
hand, and they went down the hall together.

And when they came to the door to pass out, the steward got before them and bowed as he was used to do, and he spoke very gravely to Sir Ywain, reminding him that this same afternoon had been appointed among the lords, his neighbours, for the witnessing of certain charters.

But Ywain and the boy looked at one another and laughed, and the steward saw that they laughed at the lords and at him and at the very greatness of the business: and he was enraged, and turned away and went to his new master.

Then Sir Turquin came hastily after them, and he laid his hand upon his brother's arm and bent his head a little, and spoke to him so that none else should hear, and he said: What is this that you are doing; for no man leaves all that he has, and departs suddenly, taking nothing with him. But those two went from him without answering, and they passed, as it seemed, very swiftly along the road under the woodside, and were hidden from him. And again, as he stood still watching, he saw them going swiftly above the wood where there was no path, but only the bare wold before them.

CHAPTER II.

HOW SIR YWAIN SAW HIS OWN FACE
THE FIRST TIME.

Now the truth is that when Ywain turned
his back on his old life and the snug lordship that was his, he had no thought of what
was to be the way of his wandering, nor did
he so much as know by which of the world's
four roads he would begin his journey. But
he climbed upon the open wold as if all his
pleasure was to climb and to strike his feet
firmly and to breathe deep: and the boy
went by his side in like manner, and they
spoke no word.

But when they were come to the height
of the slope, Ywain turned and looked down
upon the homestead of Sulney, and he saw

it small and clear under the midday sun, as
like as may be to a toy that a child would
play with: and there was no man moving
about it, but only the white pigeons flying
this way and that upon the roofs. And it
was lovely to him, for he saw it as a time
that is past.

Then he looked a little farther, and he saw
the broad road, and dust kindling along it
like smoke, and in the dust a great company
riding: and they rode in order by two and
by two, and their jogging was heavy, and
Ywain remembered that these were the lords
who had appointed to do business with him.

And because of them the place was no
longer lovely to him, and he turned away
and ran quickly over the ridge, and when he
could see them no more he laughed: and
the boy also ran and laughed, and their
laughter was as though they were both
truants from school, escaping narrowly with
fear and joy together. And on the other
side of the ridge they cast themselves down

upon the grass, and among the grass were thistles, and the thistles pricked them sharply, and they rolled and were pricked again, and laughed again and yet again.

Then they set their shoulders against a bank, and sat still, looking to the country that was before them. On the one hand lay the sea near by, and upon it white sails of ships that were sailing marvellously, for though they were upon the sea yet they sailed, as it seemed, high above the land. And on the other side lay a thick wood that hid all the far country, and before the wood was a village and a tower. And Ywain knew that village well enough, cot and lot, barn and balk, and he thought not at all of the village, but only of the wood and the great depth of it and of what might be beyond. And so thinking he fell asleep.

But when he awoke the sun was westering, and he looked again upon the village and saw it as though it were strange to him, and he could not remember even the name

of it. Then he stood up, and turned towards
the place beside him where the boy had
been: and as he looked he was astonished,
for the boy was there still, sleeping as himself had slept, but his face was like the face
of an old man, and the lines upon it were
countless, like bird-marks on the river sand.

So Ywain stood staring for a while, and
he said to himself: Now I know by the
trouble in my head that either I have lost
my wits, as a man beat down in battle, or
else in all this there is a meaning that I
have known and forgotten, for it seems to
be both reasonable and impossible. Then
he touched the boy's hand and awoke him,
and when he saw his eyes again, he asked
him: Who, then, are you?

And the boy said: Answer me first the
same question.

But Ywain would not, for he said: Why
must I answer first?

And the boy said: Let be, then; for you
know already what you would answer, and

there is but one and the same answer to your question and to mine.

Then Ywain looked no more into the boy's eyes but upon the ground, and bewilderment came upon him again, for he said in his heart: This that he says is madness, and yet I seem to know that it is true. And when he lifted his head again he said to the boy: How can a man speak with himself face to face: and how can I, that am neither, be both an old man and a boy?

But the boy answered him: Is not every man that which was and that which shall be: and in all the days of his life shall he not once or twice see the face of his desire? And as he spoke Ywain heard him plainly, but now he saw him not so plainly, though he stood looking down upon him in the same place: and he said quickly: Tell me this, then: what is my desire?

And he heard again the answer as one that hears a voice through the mist: but the words were in an unknown tongue. And he peered down, and stooped, and where the boy had been there was but the long grass and the thistles: and when he rose up again he saw the hillside clear before him, and the sun was low and the edges of the bents were glistening, and nothing moved among them but the wind of sunset.

CHAPTER III.

HOW IT FORTUNED TO YWAIN TO FIND A STAFF IN THE PLACE OF HIS SWORD.

THEN Ywain turned his face towards the village, and went down the hill: and he went with a good heart, for though the boy had left him, yet he hoped not to be long without him, and even now when he looked straight forward it seemed that he had the joy of his company and his laughter. But when he turned and looked beside him, there was but his own shadow; black it lay and long, and about the edges of it a brightness was shining. Then he remembered that the sun was low and night rising among the hollows, and he bethought him of his supper and sleep.

So he went quickly to the village, and

passed through it and came to the farmer's
house that lay beside the great wood : and
the farmwife gave him welcome, as one
that knew not who he was, but could well
pitch her guess within a mile or so. And
she whispered to her husband, but he was
hard of hearing and full of slumber from the
fields. So when Ywain had supped, they
showed him where he should lie. And when
he was come there he laid him down, and
the day went from him in a moment and he
knew no more whether he were alive or dead.

But very early in the morning he awoke,
and he saw that over against his face as he
lay abed there was a window in the wall. And
the window was open, and there came through
it a small sweet noise, for it was the time of
sparrow chirp, which comes just before the
rising of the sun. So he rose from his bed
and went to the window and leaned with his
arms upon the sill, watching for the day to
turn from greyness to light.

And as he leaned and watched he heard

a noise of talking in the house below, for the door was right there beneath him, and it stood open wide. Moreover, the talking was loud, for they that talked were the farmer and his wife, and she spoke loud because he was hard of hearing, and he spoke yet louder because she was his wife, and he wished his saying to prevail over hers.

So she said in a high voice: As surely as an egg is an egg, by the same token this is my lord of Sulney.

Then he spoke scornfully of her and her eggs, and he asked her for what reason of all the reasons on earth should such a one as my lord of Sulney come to sup in a farmstead that was none of his, and sleep in a vile bed, when he had better within a bare league.

And she answered quickly that though a thing were clean past a man's understanding, yet it might well happen so for all that: and further, she would have him to know that in her house were no vile beds, but such as

were fit for any man to sleep in, and she cared not who he might be.

And at that he growled a little, like a dog that is made to cease barking. Then he spoke to her again, in the manner of one who deals with a child, making a show of gentleness and mastery together. See now, he said, and I will give you three reasons why you have the wrong and I have the right of it. First then, this one that has had supper and sleeping-room of us is a young man, and quick to rise and to sit down, but my lord of Sulney is past his youth and waxing heavy. Secondly, this one came to us walking upon his own shanks, and that no lord would do that had the horses of Sulney, for I have seen them time and again, and in these parts there are none better. And beside these two reasons, there is a third that you might well have seen with your own eyes, for this man's cloak is the cloak of a pilgrim and not of a lord, and his hat and staff are such as none use but wayfarers. And if you will not believe me

now, you may ask him for the truth of it
yourself.

That will I do, said the woman.

Then Ywain fell into a study, for he saw
that in despite of all those reasons her mind
was not changed, but that she would certainly
ask the truth of him. And it seemed hard
to him to know what the truth might be:
for he remembered how he had put off the
lordship that was his, but he could not tell
how he had become young, nor how he had
lost his sword and come by the hat and
staff of his pilgrimage : so that he thought
at one moment, I am that lord, and at
another, I am not, and his life past seemed
like a dream of the night.

And while he was still wondering he went
down the steps, and in the room that was
below he saw the farmwife with bread for
him to break his fast, and the man by the
door ; and against the wall he saw his hat
and staff. And as he ate, the woman said to
him : Look you, sir, we are not used to

keep guests that are unknown to us. But
we knew you, that you are my lord of
Sulney.

Then Ywain said, I am not, and immediately the farmer slapped his hand upon his
thigh and shouted at his wife. But Ywain
saw the woman look at him, and he looked
at her, and she smiled to him as to one that
was bidding her keep a thing secret. And
she said to her husband, There is no need
for you to shout: for an apple may have a
red side and a green, and yet it is an apple,
to him that hath understanding.

Then Ywain gave her thanks, and took his
leave of them both: and he went out into
the sunlight, and followed the path into the
high wood. But he saw nothing of his way
as he went, for all his thought was upon
that answer which he had given, whereby he
had answered others, but in no wise answered
himself.

CHAPTER IV.

HOW YWAIN CAME TO AN HERMITAGE
IN A WOOD.

So Ywain marched alone in the high wood,
and for a time he saw no more the sun, nor
the light of the sun, for the wood was of
pines and they were marvellous thick above
his head. But the stems were far enough
apart and the track went this way and that
among them, and whiles it turned aside and
whiles it forked, and whiles it was no track
at all. But Ywain went always right forward
and would not stay, nor leave following his
own thought. And as he went it came again
into his mind that he was a new man, for
though he was still amazed with questions yet
he carried neither forethought nor repentance,

and he marched to a song that was in his ears. And in his marching there came to him the remembrance of the child that had led him forth, and though he knew surely that he was now alone, yet, by the imagination of his heart, he could well see the child dancing before him upon the path of the forest.

And at last when he had gone a long way and could by no means tell how long, on a sudden he looked far before him and saw the ground all fresh with grass, and no more pine-needles upon it but sunlight and shadow. And he went quickly forward and came out from the dark wood and stood in an open grove that was hoar with silver-birches: and beyond the grove was a stream that ran burbling, and beyond the stream was a bank with great beeches upon it. So for delight of that place he turned and left following the path, and went along between the beech-roots and the stream.

And as he went the bank upon the right

hand was ever higher and steeper, until there were no more beeches upon it, but by the stream was a bare lawn between this wood and that, and a little cliff thereby, as sharp as a cliff of the sea. Now the cliff was of red sand, and the face of it was carven curiously: for in it were two steps and a doorway, as it were the doorway of a church, and two windows of like fashion with a little mullion to each: so that Ywain knew it for an hermitage. And he sat down to look upon it, stepping back within the shadow of the beech-trees: and when he looked, it did him great good to see and to think upon it, for the house was small and secret, and though the carven work of it was but plain, yet it well showed the pleasure of him that had worked at it.

Then the hermit came out from within, and when he saw him Ywain kept close to watch what he would do, for he knew not the manner of hermits, nor how they live all their life-days, seeing that they have time

before them like new-fallen snow, without
fence or foot-mark.

Now the hermit had bread in his hand,
and Ywain hungered at the sight of it, for
he had had none since the morning was
early, and it was now late, and this he knew
by the hermit's shadow, for it lay small and
squat about his feet. Nevertheless he would
not move, but kept still where he sat, for his
desire to see was greater than his desire to
eat, and he thought moreover that he might
yet come to the eating after the seeing.

So he looked and saw as he desired: for
the hermit broke the bread and rubbed it
in his hand and threw the crumbs abroad
upon the lawn: and instantly there came
upon the place a dozen of small fowls, such
as dunnocks and finches, and they hovered
and hopped after the bread as long as he
would throw it. And some part of it he
would not throw, but he walked away from
the birds and came to the stream and held
out his hand above a little pool where the

water ran curdling. And Ywain knew that he was giving the remnant to the fish, and that they were by likelihood trout that came for it, for where a crumb fell upon the pool there he saw the water broken, and at some times there was no splashing but only a ridge that ran swiftly upon the face of the pool.

Then when all was finished the hermit stood looking upon the water as one that loved the sound of it and had no need to be elsewhere. But the sun was strong upon his head, and Ywain saw how he drew his hood around his neck where it was bare at the nape, and so went back to the house in the rock. And as he entered in at the doorway the shadow was cool and dark upon him, and then he was gone as a fox goes into his earth.

But Ywain mused yet a little while longer, and all that he had seen seemed strange and very good to him, like the tales of the elves and pixies, of whom there is nothing told that will not please young children, because they also have their dealing with the little things of the earth, and are of no account with grown men. And he wondered if this might be the end of his desire, to live secretly and far off from men, having his converse only with the creatures of the greenwood.

CHAPTER V.

OF THE HERMIT AND OF HIS DEALING
WITH YWAIN.

So within a while he got upon his feet and
came to the door in the rock and called to
the hermit; and the hermit came from
within and stood shading his eyes with his
hand, and asked him the reason of his calling. And Ywain answered him courteously,
making as though to take his hat from off
his head in sign of reverence: and the hermit lifted his eyes in the same moment and
saw that the hat was the hat of a pilgrim,
and yet of no accustomed pilgrim, for there
were upon it neither shells nor images.
Also he saw that Ywain's cloak was not
threadworn nor his shoes broken. And his

face he could not well see for the brightness of the sunlight, but by his voice he
might perceive him to be young and gentle,
and none of the wandering rogues of whom
all hermits dwell in dread. Then he brought
him into his cave, that was as like a house as
a cave may be, and he made him sit by a
table, and gave him to eat and to drink.

And when Ywain had well eaten and
drunk the hermit asked him concerning the
way by which he had come, and the way by
which he would go forth again : but he
would not ask of his name, nor in what
house he was born, nor even of his pilgrimage, for he also was courteous, and his
mind was to pleasure his guest and not
himself only. Nevertheless he was not
willing to lose the companionship that had
fallen to him until he should have heard
somewhat of the dealing of men, for it was
long since he had had knowledge thereof by
one of like breeding with himself. So he
spoke to Ywain of to-morrow, and of certain

things that he would show him, and Ywain
heard him gladly enough, for his feet were
now heavy with weariness and good eating.
And the hermit knew this by the sound of
his speech, and he laid him upon his own
bed and bade him take his ease.

Now when Ywain awoke he looked first
upon the wall of the chamber and saw that
there was a glint of sunlight upon it high
up, whereby he knew that the day was falling. Also he was aware that there was one
watching him, and when he had turned his
head he saw how it was the hermit who
stood in the doorway of the chamber: and
the man's face seemed to him wise and
quiet, as of one that had many thoughts
and mastery therewith.

So they two went to supper, and this was
the first time that they had eaten together.
And at one time they remembered this, and
at another they forgot it: for they spoke not
of their doing but chiefly of their deeming,
and often they would be eager the one to

put question to the other, and often they would know before question put how the answer would be.

Then at the last Ywain was minded to ask counsel of the hermit, and in one tale he told him all, to wit, how that in a day his life had changed, and how that he had left his own house and the house of his fathers, and gone out to seek his desire, and again how that he had as yet no certainty of what his desire might be. Only he told nothing of the boy that had come and led him away: but he put his own desire in place of the boy, for he was willing rather to be counted a fool than a teller of marvels. And he thought that his adventure might be judged as well by the part as by the whole, for that which he would hold back was in no wise the marrow of it.

But the hermit said: Desire is a child: yet will he take a man by the hand and lead him away.

Then Ywain was astonished, for he said

within himself, How can this hermit have
knowledge of the child, seeing that I told
him nothing?

Then the hermit said further, This is
the part of a man, to know whether his desire
be a wise child or a wayward. For the
wayward will swiftly take him a-wandering,
and swiftly in his wandering will leave him:
but the wise will never leave him utterly.

Then Ywain asked him, By what reason
may that be? And the hermit said, By
nature: for every man is that which hath
been and that which shall be.

Then Ywain was yet more astonished, and
his mind swung backwards and he thought,
Certainly I must have told him, for these
words are every one of them the words of
the boy. And instantly his mind swung
again and he thought, But I told him not.
And he looked at the hermit's face and saw
it hardly, for the twilight was covering it
from him by little and little: but he saw
the two eyes of him and they were not

fainter but clearer, and Ywain's heart lay open to them like water to the stars. And he said within himself, The words that I told not, he perceived them with his eyes.

Then the hermit rose up softly and went out, and when he came again he brought heather and fern, and he made Ywain a bed beyond his own, and they slept before it was dark.

CHAPTER VI.

YET MORE OF THE HERMIT, AND OF A WORD
THAT WAS IN YWAIN'S EARS.

In the morning when they had arisen they
went out of the house and came to the stream,
for the hermit said that they should bathe
in it, and he showed Ywain a pool that was
deep enough. Then they did off their clothes
hastily and threw themselves into the water
after the manner of otters, and at a stroke
they came to the top of the pool. And there
was a little waterfall there, and the stream
of it carried them down, and they touched
the stones and crept out upon them. Then
they took the water again more strongly
and came right to the waterfall and stood
beneath it, and it splashed upon their heads

32

and divided the hair like a cold knife. And
at that they laughed together and so threw
themselves back and were carried down
again, and they came quickly to their
clothes, blowing with their breath and shiv-
ering. But when they had run to the house
they were warm and fresh.

Then the hermit set two bowls of milk
with bread upon the table. And Ywain was
glad of the sight of that food, and he sat
where the murmuring of the stream came
in at the window, and a soft air with it,
and the world was made new for him. But
he ate and drank with few words, for he
was thinking within himself how that to-
morrow had come and he knew not yet
whether to go or stay. And often in
his thinking he looked at the hermit, and
the hermit looked kindly back at him, and
nodded: and it was as though he nodded
to Ywain's thought, but he spoke nothing
with his lips. Yet at one time there was
a voice, and Ywain heard it plainly: and

the voice said: For delight men stay, but for desire they go forth. And he looked hard at the hermit, and the hermit nodded again to him, as though he also had heard that voice, and knew it to say truth: but he spoke nothing with his lips.

Then Ywain said aloud: Surely I heard a voice and it was not your voice nor mine, yet it seemed to me that I heard it not in my imagination but in my ears.

And the hermit said: I also heard it, and before this I have heard many such, and no great wonder; for in all solitude there will be voices, as in all still water there will be visions.

And as Ywain heard those words he believed them, and he thought on still water, but found none in his remembrance: only he saw before him the picture of the stream, wherein he had but now been bathing, and the course of it was all racing and burbling, and where it lay more still, even there froth turned and drew together upon the face of it. And he asked the hermit boldly: Where then is the still water of your visions?

And the hermit answered: It is near at hand: but the looking is longer than the way thither.

CHAPTER VII.

HOW YWAIN LOOKED INTO THE WATER OF A WELL, AND OF THAT WHICH HE SAW THEREIN.

THEN they rose up and went out, and the hermit showed Ywain a little path that went along under the cliff and so into the wood beyond: and thereby, he said, was the way to a dead thorn-tree that stood in a space alone, and under the thorn-tree was a well-spring, and from the well-spring came a runnel of bright water whereby it might surely be found. Then he put a wheaten cake into Ywain's hand and said to him: Farewell now for to-day, and at supper-time come again with your visions, and we will talk of them together. But when you

stand by the well-spring and look therein, then, said he, be not weary of your looking, but return always and be always in hope until the sun go down. For the visions are not quickly to be seen, as the common sort suppose that they see all things which are before their faces: whereas they see, as it were, but the shadows upon the ground and not the life of those who cast them. But that which you seek to see is the dealing of spirits, and men come not thereto suddenly, but by long time and loneliness.

Then he returned from him, and Ywain took the path and went into the wood, and in no long space he saw a great thorn-tree before him, and it was all dead and without leaf or berry, and other trees there were none very near it, but only the cliff that bore hard upon it on the one side, whereby it leaned a little outwards. And beneath the spread of it Ywain saw a well-head made of stone from the cliff, and it was of the height of a man's thigh. Also there was a step or margin of stone under it, and the step and the well-head were both shapen with six sides, every side equal to every other, after the manner of the waxen chambers of bees. And when Ywain came nearer he saw that the spring rose in the well - head within four fingers of the brim, but it could not rise above the brim by reason of a little sluice below, that was made in the stone above the step, and a runnel came therefrom of bright water and went into the wood darkling.

Then he looked into the water of the spring, and it was deep and still, for the fountain was as great as the runnel and no more, so that there came no moving of the water that was above. But the shadow of the cliff lay yet upon the well-head, for the sun was not high, and by that reason the face of the water was like the face of a mirror, and all that Ywain could see therein was his own image, and with that the image of the thorn-tree, and no more could he see though he looked long and warily.

Aladore

So for a while he ceased from looking, and
he went into the wood beyond the well, and
walked softly therein, for he meant to come
again as the hermit had counselled him. And
as he went he mused, and when he awoke
out of his musing he perceived that the sun
was now high above him. Right so he
turned about and came quickly back to the
thorn-tree, and looked again into the water;
and where dimness had been there was sunlight, and the water was clear and thin, and
in the depth of it were many lights both
shining and shimmering, for some of them
rested in their glowing, like embers, and
some rose and curdled, like smoke of gold,
and so passed and came again continually.
But of visions Ywain could find none: only
these lights could he see, and else nothing.
Then again he left looking in the water, and
sat down under a green tree, for it was past
noon and hotter than before: and he took
his wheaten cake that the hermit had given
him and ate it sitting there. And as he

ate he thought on these days that were hardly yet three days since he left his former life, and they seemed to him to be as it were three long years, that lay between him and the time that was before.

Then suddenly he perceived that with his thinking the heat of the day had gone over, and the sun was dipped into the trees of the wood behind him where he sat. And he looked again towards the well-head that stood there before him, and a light was upon the stone of it that was the last of the sunlight, and afterwards that light passed away and the stone was left dark. Then he knew that his time was come, and he leapt up and strode to the well and leaned over it. And at the first he looked and saw nothing, for a darkness seemed to rise and roll within it, like a cloud in storm: but after no long watching the darkness rolled away, and he saw clearly.

Now that which he saw was a marvel, for it was not water, though it lay within the well-head : nor was it sunlight, for the sun was now far down behind the wood. But it was by seeming a piece of that country, as it were between the night and the day : for there was a wood and a river with a high bank, and in the sky above there was neither sun nor moon, but one only star of bright silver. And as he looked the star faded, by reason that the sky was more light, and he saw that the river was wide and shallow, and over the width of it were stepping - stones, one beyond another in a line, like floats upon a fish-net. And out of the wood came a boy, and though his face was turned away, yet could Ywain tell without doubt that he was in all things like the boy that had been with him : and his heart beat and he strained in his watching as one that fears lest he be seen or heard. But the boy came to the stepping-stones and passed lightly over them, and began to go upon the bank. And as he went there came a bright light upon the topmost of the bank, and Ywain perceived that it was the light of sunrise, and it fell upon a banner that was there, with men about it in armour, and twice or thrice there came sudden glints upon the armour. And for all that they seemed far off and small, it was clear to be seen that they fought together in two companies. And the boy, when he had climbed the bank, came to one of the companies and entered into it, and Ywain saw him no more: but that company stayed not where they were, for they were hard pushed in the fighting, and gave ground by inch and by inch. And one man of them, that had no helmet upon him, came to the edge of the bank, with a horn in his right hand: and he set the horn to his mouth to blow it, and in that instant the darkness came again, and Ywain saw nothing but only the water in the well, and the cloud that rolled within the water. And he started up, and fear and joy took him in the same blood-heat, and he turned and ran quickly by the path under the cliff.

CHAPTER VIII.

HOW THE HERMIT SET YWAIN ON HIS WAY AND OF TWO SECRETS THAT HE TOLD HIM.

Now it was the hour when the hermit would be going to supper, and thereupon came Ywain to the house. And while they sat eating and drinking Ywain told the hermit of that which he had seen: but he spoke warily, for he told him nothing of the boy.

And the hermit said: The vision is yours and not mine: yet this much concerning it is in my head and not in yours. I tell you, therefore, the woodside that was shown to you, and the stepping-stones, and the bank beyond the water, all these are of no solitary vision, but may be seen of any man that has a mind thereto.

43

Then said Ywain quickly: That mind have I; and the hermit looked him in the face and nodded to him after his own fashion. Then he told him of the way to that place which he had seen: and as he spoke Ywain saw the way plainly, as it were before him, and the winding and the turns of it, and the stars above the trees, and the setting-place of the moon. And the hermit said how it was a nine hours' yourney for a man like himself, that was now out of his youth and past hurrying.

And when he heard that, Ywain kept silence for a moment, and in the silence he made his reckoning, that it wanted even now but eight hours to sunrise. And thereupon he stood up suddenly upon his feet and stretched out his hand to bid the hermit farewell.

But the hermit left him there standing, and went to and fro and took bread from the table and put it in a wallet and brought it to Ywain, and he took also a hunting-knife from the wall behind the door, and a thong thereto, and gave it to him to belt about his middle. But Ywain laid it first upon the table, and drew the knife from out the sheath and cut off a silver button of his cloak. And the knife he returned into the sheath and left it lying: and the button he gave to the hermit in token of bargain and sale, lest in the time to come by the gift of a knife their friendship should be parted, as hath happened unto many and many. And then he belted on the knife without fear, and they two went swiftly from the house and came to the wood and entered into it.

Now the moon was high and bright, being near the full, and the light of her came softly between the trees and made clear the path. And Ywain and the hermit spoke little in their going, for all the need that they had of each other: but their speech seemed to them as it were forbidden, by reason of the shadows. So they went dumbly for the most part, walking the one before the other and making great haste, and when a full hour was gone they came to an open heath that was beyond the wood. And the hermit stayed there and set him down upon the heather, and he said to Ywain that he could go with him no farther, for the moon was fast southing and he was an hour's journey from home. But this he said courteously, as one that spoke of necessity and against his own heart.

Then Ywain sat by him, and suddenly in his heart also there came division, with thoughts straining this way and that as two hounds that strain in the same leash. For though he was hot to follow his desire, yet he remembered the companionship of the hermit and the quiet of his dwelling; moreover, he saw the man there beside him and none to take his place. But again the remembrance of the boy drew him more strongly, and he chafed till he should be gone. So he said to the hermit: Let me go now, for even as they say of death, the longer the colder, so it is with the parting of friends. But I know also that I go too soon, for you have perceived of me more than ever I told you, and of a certainty with your counsel I might have feathered my shafts. And though this may not be, yet tell me now, I pray you, in few words, of the likelihood of this my journey, how it shall prosper or in what danger it shall come, that I may thank you and fare the better.

But the hermit said: In this you are astray: for that which a man may learn in solitude is not knowledge but wisdom, and wisdom is not of this or that, but of the nature of things. So now concerning you, I know not how you shall fare, but I know of that which you may become, and in some part I know the way thereto. Follow therefore your desire, for so only can you live and be alive, and this is the first secret. But the second is this, that you serve another, for so only can you put away your enemy that was born with you. And truth it is that if a man overtake his desire and have not done away his enemy, it had been better for him that he had died first, for he shall never have peace.

And Ywain heard the words and marked them, for they were spoken deeply. But what the meaning of them should be, that he knew not yet, for his mind was all a-bubble with the thoughts of his journey and of the boy, aud of the fighting that he had seen in the vision. And the hermit perceived that he was distraught and in haste to be gone: and he stood up and bade him good-speed. But first he took a promise of him that he would come again, and then he spoke the last words and turned away into the wood.

And with that Ywain's heart fell, and his strength was slackened, and he laid his hand to the stem of a pine-tree and leaned upon it, that he might keep watch upon the hermit until he should be wholly gone from him. And at the first he saw him as a living man, but afterwards as a shadow without form or substance; for that which he saw was ever moving through the forest and the moonlight, as a fish is seen dimly in green water, going among the reeds. And at the last he saw him not at all, for the very shadow of him was wholly mingled with the night.

CHAPTER IX.

OF YWAIN'S JOURNEY BY NIGHT, AND HOW HE
WAS BROUGHT BY A LADY TO THE PLACE
OF HIS VISION, AND SO LEFT HER.

So Ywain turned him from his watching: and
as he turned him he drew his breath again,
and his heart rose and he took the path
strongly among the heather. And he went
therein a good two hour or more, until he
saw upon his left side how the land rose up
ridgewise like the back of a great hog: and
for all that it was night, yet he saw the top
of the ridge clearly, as it were a black line
that ran along the sky. And thereover stood
the moon all broad and yellow, and he perceived that this was the place of her setting,
as the hermit had shown it to him by his

counsel. Then he knew that it was hard on midnight, and he had great gladness because that he had come so far on his way and no time lost. And he left the heath and took a good road that was below the ridge, and for a little space the moon hung above him as it were a great lantern of yellow horn. And then she sank behind the ridge, and in no long time afterwards the land was dark.

Nevertheless he ceased not to go swiftly and without stumbling, for the stars were now brighter before him, and the road under his feet was smooth and white with dust, so that he had no need to walk warily. And as he went he remembered all the words of the hermit, and he turned them over in his mind as a man turns over his money upon his hand: for it may chance that he knows not yet how much it is, or in what manner it may serve him. Even so Ywain considered the words of the hermit, and namely the two secrets: whereof one was plain to his understanding and one was dark. For he was of himself fully minded to follow his desire; but to serve another was no such matter, seeing that in his old life he had served both lords and over-lords, and for his wages had little but weariness. And in this wise he reasoned hotly as he went, speaking as it might have been to the hermit himself there present.

Then upon the instant his sight went from him, as it happens many times to those that reason hotly. And he saw no more the road beneath him nor the stars above, but by seeming he came again into the house in the rock, and there was the hermit sitting over against him, and his eyes shining in the twilight. And Ywain said to the hermit: What is this secret that you have told me, and how can a man both follow his desire and also serve another? For by his desire he would be free, but service is to freedom as water upon fire. And the semblance of the hermit looked at him and nodded kindly, but he answered nothing to Ywain's questioning, save that he spoke again the former words.

Then because of the hermit's voice and the deepness of it and the quiet of his house, the tangle in Ywain's heart was untwisted and he had no more lust of reasoning.   And he came back as it were from another place, and perceived that he had been a long time absent, for the way was changed beneath his feet, and from being a high-road was become a green ox-drove, and the stars in the sky were few and pale.

Then Ywain saw that the night was far gone, and fear came suddenly upon him lest in his dreaming he should have wandered aside from the right way.   And he stood still to peer about him, but he could see nothing save only the ox-drove and a little bank that was the border of it, and the field beyond the border.   But while he stood still there came the sound of a cock crowing: and in the same instant he was aware of a tower that lay hard by, and it lay in the field all bare and open where he had looked before and had seen nothing, until the crowing of the cock. But now he could see it without peering, and how it stood on a little mound in the field, with a pool beside it and a great rowan-tree thereby.

Then he made to go to the tower, and when he came to the bank to pass out of the ox-drove he found a gate therein: and he looked over the gate and saw how there was a door opened in the tower, and a woman that came out from it, and she began to go towards him over the field. So he passed through the gate and went out to meet her. And as he went he perceived that she was some great one, for she was richly arrayed in colours all of blue, and her raiment was close about her as the sheath is about a flower. Also she wore a veil and not a hood, and the veil was upon her head only and not upon her face, and it was light and cloudy like smoke in still air.

And when they two drew together the lady bade Ywain good-morrow, and great wonder took hold upon him: for her voice came to

him as it had been out of old memory, and
whereas in her outward seeming there was
nothing that was not strange to him, yet by
her speaking he was persuaded heartily that
he had known her all the years of his life.
Then she asked him whither he went, and he
began to tell her of the place of the stepping-
stones and of the fighting beyond the water.
And she heard him courteously, but while he
spoke she ceased not to go forward, so that in
short time they came again to the bank and
the ox-drove.

And Ywain looked before him in the half-
light, and again he was amazed: for the gate
was there by which he had passed out, and
beside it were two horses, a white and a
black, and by their bridle-reins they were
tethered to this post and to that. Then the
lady came to the white horse, and she laid her
hand upon the mane of him, and her one foot
she gave into Ywain's hand and so went to
saddle and rode fast away. And Ywain took
the black horse and followed hard after her:

and they rode long and the sky lightened towards dawn, and they went ever faster and faster, till the wind rushed by their faces as a stream rushes by the stakes of a weir.

So they came to a wood and coasted it, for the trees of it were set so thick together that no horse might go therein : also the land fell sheer and sudden within it. And in a five furlongs more the lady stayed her galloping, and she leapt down and cast away her bridle-rein and turned her into the wood. And Ywain followed after her, and she caught him by the hand, and they two ran down the wood together with pain and stumbling. And they came to the edge of the wood, and the land there was level, and Ywain looked out between the trees and saw the place of his vision, for there before him was a meadow and a broad water with stepping-stones, and beyond the water was a bank. And upon the top of the bank there went a banner, with men fighting about it : but child there was none to see, neither upon the stones neither upon the bank.

Then Ywain raged within himself to go
forward, but first he turned him of his
courtesy to give thanks to the lady, for he
said that without help of her he had never
come there: whereby he was wholly bounden
to her, if that she would command him in
anything. And she looked him in the eyes
and said to him: Yea, sir, are you so
bounden? Then have I found a friend to
my need: for I have a hundred knights that
are sworn of my allegiance, yet there is none
of them that serveth not his own desire before
mine.

Then despair came upon Ywain, as upon a
wild thing that is trapped, and he struggled
blindly and saw no way out. And in his
struggling he heard the sound of a horn that
was blown behind him, and he turned about
and perceived him that blew it standing upon
the height of the bank. And at the blare of
that horn all the blood of his body was made
fire, and he left the lady alone and went
furiously up to go into the battle.

CHAPTER X.

OF THE LADY AITHNE, AND OF THE GIFTS THAT SHE HAD FROM HER BIRTH.

Now leave we Ywain to his fighting and turn we to the lady, that was there heavily cast down to be so left and benothinged. For she was of all earthly women the most beautiful and the wisest in magic: yet she had great need of such as would serve her truly, for her life was full of pain and perplexity, being divided in a strange manner between two realms. And this came of no sudden hap, but it fortuned so to her from her birth, and was according unto her nature, as I shall show you.

First then, she was of a high lineage and descended out of faery: for her father was Sir

Ogier, Lord of Kerioc, that lies over beside Broceliande, and her mother was called the Lady Ailinn of Ireland, and she came of the kindred of Fedelm of the Sidhe, that was called Fedelm of the Nine Shapes, by reason that she could take on her nine shapes, and each more beautiful than other. Therefore the Lady Ailinn would have called her daughter Fedelma, but Sir Ogier named her with the name of Aithne, and she was called thereby all her life-days, as for her earthly name : but of her elfin nature she had other names, as was but reason, and in especial one name she had that none ever knew but Ywain only. So of that name I shall make no more matter.

Now when the Lady Ailinn had been some while wedded, and was looking for her child to be born presently, upon a night she lay abed in the castle of Kerioc : and midnight was two hours past and there was none waking but that lady alone. And in her chamber was a fire of wood burning, for the year was still

cold and hard : and the fire was bright and
cast upon the wall of the chamber both light
and shadow. And Ailinn lay so upon her bed
that she saw not the window, but the wall
only, and she perceived that the shadow upon
it was the shadow of her nurse, that was fallen
asleep beside the hearthstone.

Nevertheless though the nurse slept, yet were
there voices in the chamber, as of two women
beside the fire : and Ailinn knew well that
they were fays, or women of the Sidhe,
seeing that there were upon the wall no
shadows of them but only of the nurse. So
she lay still to hearken what they would say.
And one said: The child shall be a woman,
and I give her the gifts of womanhood : for her
skin shall be white as the swans of Aengus,
and her eyes grey like the dawn, and the colour
of her cheeks soft like the sunset. And she
shall be loved by a hundred knights and one,
and her love shall be to her true lover both
meat and madness, like the wild honey of
Arroy: and so is my giving done. And the

other said : The child shall be a fay, and I give her the gifts of faery : for she shall hold of me the realm of Aladore, that was the Rhymer's heritage : and of her own magic she shall come thereto and therefrom, all her days. And so is my giving done.

Then the two voices fell silent, and Ailinn turned her upon her bed that she might see after what likeness they were that had spoken. And she saw no one by the fire save the nurse only. But in that moment came the moon, going downwards to the sea, and a beam of her shining entered into the chamber and lay upon the floor, and so moved across the floor and came to the hearthstone. And in that beam Ailinn saw plainly how there stood two shapes of women between the bedside and the hearth. And they were grey shapes and thin as air, for she saw behind them the fire burning and the embers of it, but she saw it some deal faint, as it were behind two wisps of smoke.

Then those two fays drew near to her
and stood by the bedside, and the one
of them touched her head and the other
touched her hand. And at the touch of
them her blood was made heavy, and she
slept deep, beyond voice or vision. And in
the morning when she awoke she found in
her hand a golden key, and upon her head
she found also a golden comb that she
knew not: and by the tokens of the key
and the comb she had certainty of that
which she had heard and seen. But of
the meaning thereof she held great debate
with herself and might not be satisfied.
And she thought to take counsel of her
kindred, when she should come again into
Ireland: but to Sir Ogier, that was her
husband, she said nothing of the matter,
for he was a man that had no dreams,
neither by night, neither by day.

Then in short space thereafter the child
was born, that was called Aithne, and she
was heir to her father and her mother both,

for other child they had none, man nor maid, but this one only. And she was a wise child and a beautiful, but always she made for herself a way and walked in it. And when she was come to seven year, and it was the day of her birth, she played in the Castle of Kerioc all such games as she would. And at the last she came into her mother's chamber and there found a little chest, and opened it, and in the chest was a comb of gold and a key of the same. And the key she left there lying, but the comb she laid into her hair, and stood before a mirror and preened herself. Then came her mother suddenly and took the comb from her, and gave her instead the key of gold, to make her a game therewith. And right so the child was gone from the place, and she was seen no more in Kerioc for the space of three hours. Then before night she came again with the like swiftness, and she was no whit weary or hungry or afeared, but she greeted her mother

dearly as one that had been long gone
from her into a far country. And afterwards the child said how that she had been
in Aladore, and the time that she had been
there was by her deeming three years, for
she said firmly that she had seen the cow-
slips there three several times, and three
times had gathered them all fresh in their
springing. And thereat her father laughed
out, as a man will laugh that hath the
better knowledge: but the Lady Ailinn perceived that she spoke truth. And as the
child had said, so it was with her many
times thereafter: for she came and went by
her own magic, and that was by the gift
that she had of faery.

CHAPTER XI.

THEN with the years so passing the time
came that Aithne was a damsel grown, and
many knights sought her love and many
asked to have her in marriage. And it
happened at this time that her mother, the
Lady Ailinn, was taken with sickness, and
though her malady was but light to the
deeming of such as saw her and heard her
speak thereof, yet inwardly she knew that
the end of it was to be by death only.

So upon a day she lay in her chamber in
the Castle of Kerioc, and Aithne sat there
beside her and they talked together of this

and of that. And at the last the Lady Ailinn ceased from talking, and then she spoke to Aithne again and said: My daughter, I would not have you parted from me by blindness, as others are parted from me: for they deem that in the Spring I shall be healed of this my malady, whereas I know inwardly that before the thorn is hoar I must be otherwhere. And of that, beloved, I say no more; for you too shall one day pass out by this gate, and I bid you to the Tryst after Death. But as for your earthly life I have a counsel for you: that you consider well to whom you give yourself; seeing that a woman should not love but after her own kind, and for one such as you are this may well be a hard thing to compass. For the half of your heart is with the faery, and the half of your days you live in a land that is no land of men. And of that land I also have had knowledge, for I was somewhile there in my maidenhood: and though I came never there again, yet have I remembered it in my dreams, and I know this, that few men find the way thereto. Yet will a maiden think, as I also thought, to take a man for lord and lover and to bring him in thither: but the magic of it is not so, for every man must win there by his own desire. Choose then whom you will, as of your sovranty: but if it may be, my daughter, before your choice be uttered, come you up hither into this that was my chamber, wherein also you were born, and remember me, and how that I spoke with you of that realm that is your heritage. So shall your choice be my choice, for good fortune or for ill, and we two shall not be parted.

Then Aithne when she heard those words held her mother fast by the hand and bowed her head down upon the pillow beside her: and she wept bitterly, for the heart of youth cannot bear to hear speak of death and departing. And it is no marve., seeing that the darkness is great and the Tryst is very far off. So it was with Aithne at her mother's departing; for in no long time afterwards that lady's life failed her, as in this world, and she was gone. But Sir Ogier for all his grief was still the more minded to make for his daughter some marriage of good counsel: for he held women to be as it were ships, that may fetch and carry well enough, but without a master they are blown about and go no whither.

Now came again those knights of whom I spoke before: and they were by number a hundred from the first to the last. And they loved her all of them, not for her lands only, but each with such love as he had: for her beauty some, and some for her sweet voice, for oftentimes when she spoke and looked the blood would dance in them that heard her. And many there were that came from far countries, whereof some sought her for the praise that went abroad of her, even to the out isles, and some for the renown of her father Sir Ogier; for he was a great knight under shield, and a hunter that never knew weariness, and thereby he came quickly to his end, for he took the river with a horse that was wholly spent.

So Aithne was left alone, and her loneliness was great: for always in her castle of Kerioc she saw the faces of them that were otherwhere, and at night she had no peace for the crying of the sea-birds. And many times she made escape into her realm of Aladore: but there also was loneliness, for she had found as yet no soul to dwell with her. I speak not of fays, for of them there was great plenty: but they have no comfort in them, for they are born of moonlight and not of blood and breath. Therefore also they are from the beginning without transgression, and they know not pain or memory, neither do they fear or hope at all. And of these Aithne took no count, save that she dwelt often with them and was their lady in Aladore. But of the knights that were her earthly servants she took much pleasure and perplexity: and to one or another of them she came near to have yielded her.

Yet when the time came, at every time she held aback: for she remembered her mother the Lady Ailinn and the promise that she made to her at her departing, and always when she thought of her words she saw that they were true. And therewith she remembered a saying of her father, and she saw that this also was true, as for the most part: for he said of men and women that though they be born of one blood yet they are ever strangers each to other, both by kind and by custom, and though they sit at one board and lie under one blanket, yet they dwell apart all their lifedays. But Aithne hated that saying in her heart, and in her hope she bettered it.

CHAPTER XII.

OF THE WARRING OF TWO COMPANIES, AND HOW YWAIN DID BATTLE FOR THE ONE OF THEM AGAINST THE OTHER.

MARK now that which I tell you concerning the Lady Aithne: for after the manner of minstrels I tell you both that which she knew herself and that which she knew not. First then she knew not, for all her magic, that this was a man of a strange fortune, and as it were born again by the casting away of his possessions: nor she knew not yet what her spirit and his spirit had perceived at first sight, each of other. But she knew in her heart darkly that he was either boon or bane to her, for of his coming she had been warned without words, as it will happen to those that have the gift: and this also darkly, that his looking and his speaking were both to her mind, whereby she was the more cast down at his breaking from her. And again she knew not wherefore he should wish to go, yet she could not choose but remember that he seemed to have some great purpose in his going; and upon a man's face such purpose will show like beauty, so that even out of her pain there grew a sweetness, as fruit grows out of the wounding of a tree.

But Ywain thought not at all of her, neither darkly nor clearly, for he saw the banner upon the top of the bank and under it the two companies fighting. And they fought in a green ground before the gate of a city: and they that fought to keep the city were all of a likeness, armed every one in black armour, and their banner was of black with a golden tower upon it. But they that strove against them were furnished scantily and piecemeal, no two

alike, save that every man of them had a
sword in his hand, and upon his body a
badge of a silver scutcheon with an eagle
displayed therein, and though the badges
were of one fashion yet they were of diverse
colours.

Now when Ywain came to the top of
the bank he saw the companies, and the city
some deal beyond them, and he looked about
him to see the boy, and saw nothing of him.
But hard by there was a man there standing, the same that had blown upon the horn,
and beside his feet upon the grass lay two
naked swords. And as Ywain looked towards
him he threw down his horn and took up
the two swords, and the one of them he
gave into Ywain's hand, and the other he
took by the hilt, and without a word said
they two began running towards the banner,
for it was some way from the bank thereto.
And when they were come there where the
banner was, Ywain saw that the companies
had ceased from fighting and were standing

apart: and they were glad to do so, as he guessed, by reason that the men of the Tower were weary and fordone with the burden of their armour, and as for the men of the Eagle they were beaten back, and there were many of them wounded and some dead men. But the battle in this manner standing still, there came forth a man of the Tower armed at all points, and he mocked the men of the Eagle for striplings and fools, and defied them to fight with him, man to man and one down another to come on.

Then when Ywain heard those proud words it seemed to him as though the quarrel were his own quarrel and the scorn the scorn of his proper enemy: for he looked upon the company of the Eagle and saw them as men, enduring with weariness and pain, but those of the Tower he saw not as human flesh but as ironwork of artificers, multiplied according to one pattern, and without blood or mercy in them: and he hated them and the green earth went red before his eyes.

Then again his blood changed, and his heart became hard and smooth and cool like the heart of oak: and he stooped slowly and took from a dead man the badge that he had worn, and made it fast upon him, and he threw down his cloak and in his left hand he took the knife that the hermit had given him, and in his right hand the sword. And he stepped forward until he came within five paces of his enemy, and the two companies drew near to watch the fighting, and the man of the Tower let close his visor and came on. And Ywain looked at him and saw how he moved him as one that bears a great weight and under-props it warily lest it fall over on this side or on that: and he remembered to have moved himself in like manner at end of day, when he was outwearied in the wars. And he laughed in his heart at the remembrance, for it seemed to him of good counsel. And in that moment he saw his enemy make at him to strike, and he caught the stroke upon his sword and put it by, and ran in upon him as dog runs in upon dog, and caught him by the throat and shook him one way with his arms and another way with his knee, and threw him down upon the ground.

Then the man of the Tower rolled heavily in his armour, that he might come to his knees and rise again, but in his rolling Ywain fell upon him and pressed him down, so that he grubbled in the earth with his visor as a swine grubbles with his snout. And Ywain held him so and leaned upon him: and he struggled with his legs a little, but no long time, for his breath left him. Then Ywain found the lace of his helm, and with the hermit's knife he cut it, to recover him: and in the cutting of it he was aware of a great shouting and ramping all about him; and he looked up and saw that the men of the Eagle had run in upon those of the Tower even as he had run in upon his man, and had toppled them in like manner, and they were prising them open with their swords, whereby in short space they had them all unharnessed and disarmed.

Then Ywain got him to his feet, and the rest in like wise: and they of the Eagle gave the banner into Ywain's hands and set him in the forefront, and they marshalled the men of the Tower as beaten men behind him, and so set forth with shouting towards the city.

CHAPTER XIII.

HOW YWAIN WAS BROUGHT INTO THE CITY
OF PALADORE.

WELL may you imagine that Ywain was
astonished as he went, for it came upon
him coldly that he knew not what he had
done, nor wherefore, and moreover he saw
that he had not yet come to the end of the
matter. And he would willingly have ques-
tioned those that went with him, but they
were every man of them a-bawling and
a-singing, and when he spoke to them they
answered nothing to the purpose, but continued praising him and giving him joy. And
so with great tumult they came before the
gate of the city, and there was Ywain yet
more astonished, for he had thought to find

it well shut and defended. But now the barriers were down and the gate was open, and upon the gatehouse and upon the walls there stood a multitude of people past counting, and they cried: An Eagle! an Eagle! and shouted for joy every man louder than another.

Then Ywain and they that were with him entered the gateway and passed through it, and began to go into the city. And certain of the townsfolk took the banner from between Ywain's hands and carried it before him; and others of them pressed upon the beaten men of the Tower and jeered at them by their names and cast dust upon their heads: and so they came all together to the market - place, which was great and square, but the crowd of them filled it from side to side and from end to end, and stood therein as close as standing barley.

Now on one side of the market-place was a high hall, with steps thereto; and those that led Ywain brought him to the steps and

made him stand there upon a width of stone
where he could be seen of all, and the multitude threw up their hands and waved them
at him, crying that he should speak to them.
And this he would have done willingly, as
one not unused to speak before others, but
what he should find to say to these men,
that he could no more tell than a babe
unborn, for he was alone in a strange world,
and the time of his understanding was not
yet begun. Moreover, though the secret of
Solomon had been in his mouth, yet he
could not have uttered it for the noise of
the shouting, which came about him like the
clamouring of rooks when they are fluttered,
and so continued for the space of a good
hour. And an evil hour it was for him,
seeing that the sun was now high and fierce,
and the burden of it made his back weary,
and the noise became as it were a bruise
within his head.

And at the last, when it was now hard on
noon, he saw that the crowd was moved

and parted to right and left, and through the midst there came a train of great ones, walking slowly between halberdiers and trumpeters. And they came upon the steps of the great hall, where Ywain was standing, and saluted him with bowing; and two that were servants brought him a robe of black, broidered with gold, and they made as though they would have taken from him his cloak of pilgrimage. But that he would by no means suffer, for he remembered how he had come by it: so that in the end they covered his cloak with the robe and were content. Then two of the chief ones took him by the hand and led him into the great hall, and there went in after them all that train and many more.

CHAPTER XIV.

HOW YWAIN SAT AT FEAST IN PALADORE WITH THE COMPANY OF THE TOWER AND THE COMPANY OF THE EAGLE.

Now the hall was ordered within as for a feast, and the ordering of it was after the accustomed manner of feasts: for at one end of it was a high table upon a däis, and other two tables there were that came squarely therefrom as the two posts of a door come squarely from the lintel. And the napery upon the tables was fine and white, and the dishes were of silver: but upon the däis was a cupboard, and the cups upon it and the ewers and the plates were all of gold. And up and down the hall there went six marshals who showed courteously to each man where he should be seated: and they showed to

Ywain a seat at the high table, and when
he sat therein he overlooked wellnigh all the
hall. Then came two pages with water to
let wash his hands, whereof he thanked them
without feigning. Then the marshals brought
to him those that should sit on either side
of him, and when they had demanded of
Ywain how he should be called, then they
named each to other by their names. And
of those two the one was called Sir Rainald,
and he was shaped like a pear and yellowed
in face, and slow of speech as one upon
whom men wait: and about his neck was a
gold chain, and a jewel of gold hung thereby,
made in the fashion of a tower. But the
other of them was by name Hubert, and he
was a young man and slight; and he bore
upon him the scutcheon of the Eagle, and
his speech was restless and full of joy.

Then stood up a great Archbishop, and a
herald smote upon the table and called loudly
for silence: and when the Archbishop had
spoken a set piece of grace, then all men
stirred and sat them down again with much

clatter. And thereupon came servitors and
served every man with meat and drink.

And as Ywain ate and drank his weariness
departed and his spirit came again to him,
and he was minded to learn the truth of all
that he had seen that day. To which end
he turned him first to Sir Rainald, seeing
that he was manifestly of the Tower and
dwelt, as Ywain supposed, within the city.
But Sir Rainald was not to be so handled:
for he was such an one as would liever ask
ten questions than answer two, and his
manner of speaking was like water that is
slow and deep, against which there is no
force to stand, but only to go therewith. Yet
was the man courteous after his kind, for
he said how that Ywain had done well, as
for so young a fighter, and might yet come
to some good. And though he knew it not,
yet in one matter he told Ywain that which
he would have asked him: for when he began
to speak he demanded to know this, whether
Ywain had been in Paladore at any time past,
or was only that day come among them. And

thereby Ywain perceived that the name of the city was called Paladore.

Then in no long time weariness came again upon Ywain, and he left speaking with Sir Rainald, making excuse in the best manner that he could : and he set his hope upon the young man Hubert, for he saw that he bore the scutcheon of the Eagle. And Hubert told him all that he asked, and more thereto : for he said that what was done was done according to the custom of the city, whereby each year they banished all such of the young men as had come to their strength : and once in each year the young men came before the gate in a company and demanded to enter, and they were favoured of many within the city, but certain of the elders went out and fought with them to drive them away. And this they did because of the company of the Tower : for it was a most ancient company, and they feared greatly lest the young men should change the ordinance thereof, seeing that it was fitter for men in age than in youth.

Then Ywain asked him concerning the

company of the Eagle, and first, what was
the ordinance of it: and Hubert said that
they had no ordinance but one, and that was
that every man should wear his own colours
and do after his own heart: and this also,
that he should always and in all places fight
against the Tower. Then Ywain asked him
again whether it was so that the Eagles had
always the better of the Tower, as they had
at this present. And Hubert said that there
was no such fortune: for though they were
many in number and of a great spirit, yet
they were poor and poorly furnished: and
there was yet another reason, and that was
because they kept no fellowship together and
had small knowledge of war. For as soon
as one of them gathered skill or strength
in fighting, they of the Tower came secretly
and offered him entrance, so that for the
time to come he fought not against them.
Yet, time and again, he said, there would
come one that could not be reckoned with; so
that once in ten years, as it might be, the

Eagles would have the mastery; and for the hope of such an one the horn was blown, to call him to the place of the fighting.

Then Ywain left that, lest he should seem to speak of himself, and he said how he was astonished because that he saw about him both those of the Eagle and those of the Tower, sitting and feasting together after so cruel a day's work. And Hubert answered that this also was of the custom, and great was the evil that came of it: for though a young man, he said, may become old before his time, never will an old man come back into the mind of his youth, so that it was but according with nature that through the mingling of the companies the Tower should be continually plenished and the Eagles minished.

Then the herald called again for silence, and Ywain and Hubert spoke no more together. And when the Archbishop had chanted yet another piece then all men went out from the hall.

CHAPTER XV.

OF THE GIFTS THAT WERE GIVEN TO YWAIN
AND OF A DREAM THAT HE DREAMED.

AND it was now long past noon, but the crowd continued still in the market-place, and when they saw Ywain come out upon the steps they shouted again : for above all things they loved to see fighting and to hear tell of it. Also they were glad when they saw the Eagle go before the Tower : for men will reverence their betters and yet take pleasure to see them discomfited ; moreover they of the Tower ruled continually over them and were thereby the heavier to bear, but they of the Eagle came only to make sport for them.

Ywain therefore perceived that the commons held him in honour of their own good will: but the great ones he deemed to be his friends in fear rather than in love, honouring him for the sake of the custom and because he had the good will of others. Nevertheless they spoke not so but continued in their courtesy: for they set him in the midmost of their train and brought him through the city to a house that was made ready for him, and the house and all that was in it they gave him freely to have and to hold. Furthermore they gave him certain customary gifts in such case provided: and first, a hogshead of wine, very sweet and very drowsy, and this was the gift of the Eagles; and second, a silver collar, that all men might salute him whensoever they saw it, and this was the gift of them of the Tower, for they themselves loved such greeting beyond measure. And the third gift was a full bushel of gold, and this was the gift of the whole city and the greatest of the three, for in Paladore they have a saying that gold is the noblest of the metals, and nobleness they honour above all virtues. Then when they had given Ywain these gifts, they took their leave of him, as for that time : and Ywain thanked him as best he might, and made fast the door of his house. And for a short space he was content to look about him at one thing and another, as a child will play with his toys when they are new : and then he thought to taste of the wine that had been given him, and when he had drawn a little of it into a cup, he drank it. And for a moment he had some joy thereof, for it was sweet upon the tongue and ran bravely through his blood : but afterwards the drowsiness in it was yet stronger than the sweetness and the bravery, so that he desired no more to live but only to dream, and instantly he had his desire.

Now in his dream it seemed to him that he awoke out of sleep and saw that the sun was set and the moon rising. And in the moonlight he saw beside him a boy weeping, and it was the boy whom he had followed and found not. Then Ywain had great pain

at the heart, and he asked him the reason
of his weeping: and the boy gave him no
word, either of reason or unreason, but continued weeping pitifully. So for comfort
Ywain took him by the hand: and instantly
the boy left weeping, and made to go forth,
and he led Ywain from the house as formerly
he had led him from the house of Sulney.

Then they two went through the streets
together and came quickly to the gate of
the city, that was the same by which Ywain
had come in: and the gate was shut and
locked, and the porter gone within the gatehouse. But the boy laid his hand against
the wicket and opened it lightly, and he drew
Ywain after him, and they went out towards
the place of the fighting. And the boy
stayed not there, but went forward to the
edge of the steep bank and looked towards
the wood: and Ywain also looked with him,
and he saw the river and the stepping-stones
and the meadow-ground beyond them. And
by the woodside was a poplar tree new fallen,

and thereon he saw under the moon that
lady sitting, and suddenly in his dream he
repented him that he had so left her, and
he well knew wherefore the boy had wept.
And they two ran down to her together and
Ywain cast himself before her: and he laid
his hands between her hands and sware by
his faith to serve her truly. And in his dream
she looked kindly upon him, and he saw
her eyes, and they were grey like the dawn,
and filled with coming brightness. So he
turned him about to bring in the boy, that
he also might be comforted: but the place
was all clear moonlight, and boy there was
none, neither to right nor to left.

Then the lady rose up and went towards
the city of Paladore: and Ywain went with
her, and she brought him to the gate and
it was shut. But with her hand she touched
the wicket and so opened it, and they entered
in thereat. And in short space they came
to Ywain's house and passed it by, and when
they had gone some deal farther they came

before a house that Ywain knew not, where was a great shield of arms beside the doorway. And there the lady stayed, and she looked at Ywain, and he at her, and when he thought that she would have said somewhat she turned her away: and she went from him into the house without word spoken. Then Ywain also went his way: and as he went in his dream the moon set, and the sun rose on Paladore.

CHAPTER XVI.

HOW YWAIN FOUND HIS LADY AGAIN, AND HOW SHE WENT FROM HIM THE SECOND TIME.

LONG time was Ywain musing on that which had befallen him by night, and it seemed to him that he had been made to live as it were in two lives, seeing that out of one sleep he had twice awaked. And of the truth of this he had no certainty, but of his service that he had sworn to his lady, of that he had certainty, for whether in his dream or out of his dream his heart assented thereto. Moreover, he desired greatly to come again to that house where he had seen her go from him: and if such a house there were in Paladore, he doubted not to find it, for he saw yet

before his eyes the shield of arms that was
there beside the door, and it was party of
sable and silver, with a ship sailing therein
counter-coloured.

But now while he was musing came a
messenger from Sir Rainald, and entreated
him of his courtesy that he would be with Sir
Rainald shortly, for he had that to say to
Ywain which was worth his hearing. So
Ywain went with the messenger and came to
Sir Rainald. Then Sir Rainald spoke to him
slowly and with many words, as men speak of
grave matters: and he told Ywain how he
was commanded to bring him that same day
before the Prince of Paladore, and he gave
him joy therewith, for he said that the honour
was great, and such as fell not commonly to
them that were strangers, but if they were
on some embassage.

Then Ywain thanked him in such words as
were fitting, and so covered his thought: for
in his old life he had had knowledge of princes
and he was well-a-way weary even to remember

them. Yet for the desire that he had to meet again with his lady, and to do her service, he was willing to pleasure Sir Rainald and the Prince and any other. So when an hour had been set, that he should meet with Sir Rainald before the door of the Great Gard, then Ywain took his leave and was gone until the evening.

And first he came hastily to his own house: for before any other thing that he might do he was set to find that house of the shield, and he thought to go by the way of his dream. And he found the way like as he remembered it, and came before the house and saw the shield: and he entered into the house, for the door was unlatched and there was no man to stay him or to answer him. Yet he entered not so easily, for the door stood heavy against his hand and cried out upon him: and he perceived that the hinges of it were eaten with old rust. Also upon the inward side of it was much cobweb of spiders, and in the hall-way dust like grey sand upon the flags. Then he went from chamber to chamber, and they were all wide and waste in like manner: and his eyes were darkened to look upon the place, and his heart was cold within him, for he saw it as a place of the dead that was mouldering and forgotten.

Then at the last he came into a little chamber that was high above the hall: and it was the chamber of all the house that was most richly hung and furnished, and in it was a lute and a book and a frame of broidery, and upon the wall a round mirror of glass. And he came to the mirror and stood still to look into it, and when he looked the blood leapt in his heart as a horse leaps to the spur: for in the glass was the chamber made small and clear, as it were far off, and all things in order as he had seen them, save only that before the frame of broidery he saw a lady sitting at the work. And for all the bending of her head and the shadow upon her, he knew well that she was his own lady; and he kept watch upon her where he stood, for to move him from the mirror he dare not, lest she should go from him again.

Then he saw in the glass how she raised her head, and looked: and in that same instant the mirror was filled with cloud, and he turned him swiftly about in great fear. But his fear was vain, for his lady was verily there before him sitting, and by her the book and the lute, and all things in the chamber. And she gave him no greeting, but bent still to her broidery and made as though he had been long time there with her. And presently she bade him take the lute and sing thereto: and her voice was light and careless, as of one that thought most of her own business.

Then he was ashamed, for he had no skill with the lute, and he prayed her forgiveness humbly. Then she said it was no matter, but that he should take the book and read to her. And he took the book, and opened it: but every word that was in it was written in an unknown tongue, so that he was ashamed for this time also. Then again she said it

was no matter, but for a little while she was silent : and afterward she bade him look from the window and tell her of that which he saw. So he came to the window, that was an oriel and high above ground : and before it and beneath lay the ridge tiles of the city, and beyond them was a wall with battlements, and above the battlements was a long line and dim, where the sky met with the sea.

Then he said to his lady, I see some part of the city hereunder, and what shall I say of it to do you pleasure ? But she answered him that he should look not upon the city, but beyond it. Then he said to her, I see above the battlements a dimness of blue, and in it is a line where the sky meets with the sea : and what more shall I say of it to do you pleasure ? And she answered him not, but left her broidering and so came and stood beside him at the window, and they two looked upon the sea together. And at the last she said to him, Look well now and tell me all : for I see that of which you have not told me. And he looked again, shading his eyes with his hand and peering carefully: but nothing could he see, save one dimness upon another.

Then an evil thought came into his mind, and he said within himself, This is her will, to put shame upon me, and to make me speak of that which I see not, as though I saw it with my eyes. Then he looked once again, and as he looked he spoke, and in his voice was a little grain of anger, as small as the sand that grits between the teeth. And he said, I see nothing where nothing is: and in that instant he heard his lady sigh, there as she stood beside him; and sorrow came upon him to hear her, and he would have turned to yield himself. And he turned and found her not, for in the taking of a breath she was gone from him.

CHAPTER XVII.

OF ALADORE AND OF THE SANDS CALLED THE SHEPHERDINE SANDS.

THEN Ywain groaned inwardly, for he said, I am a fool and worse than a fool, and for a moment he hated himself and all that he had done. But afterward he considered a little and said, This comes not of folly but of newness, for I have not been used to live in two several lives. Yet by all seeming my lady does even so, and I with her: therefore she knew well that I was her sworn servant, dream in and dream out, and if I had bethought me of this I had never been angry. But now I have offended the second time, and how I am to meet with her again I cannot tell, seeing that she comes and goes like the wind among the leaves.

So he went down the house and out of it, and set his face to go toward the sea, for he thought by carefulness or by good hap he might come to perceive that which before had been hid from him. And as he went he heard one call him by his name, and he looked about and saw the young man Hubert behind him coming quickly, and he stayed for him so that they went forward together. And as they went they talked, and this time also Hubert told Ywain all such things as he demanded to know, for whether feasting or fasting he was ever the same man, and his speech was restless and joyful.

And first Ywain asked him of the house of the shield, wherefrom he had come; and Hubert said that it was of old the house of Sir Ogier, but now of his daughter the Lady Aithne, for Sir Ogier was by his own out-rageousness drowned and dead. And of the Lady Aithne he said that she was beautiful beyond telling, and therein Ywain well believed him, and then he said that she came never there, but hated them of Paladore and forsook them utterly, and Ywain laid that saying by, that he might ponder it.

Then in their talking they came to the wall of the city, and Ywain saw before him a gate that he knew not yet: and beside it upon the left hand was a castle, and a courtyard, and men afoot with halberds, and men ahorse with swords drawn, and many folk coming and going. And this, said Hubert, is the Great Gard of the Prince of Paladore, and it lies against the wall of the city and overtops it, and so runs a good furlong to the south: but on the east it stands above the city and looks down into it, as a tree may stand above a sheep-fold. Yet not so in truth, for in what place a tree stands, there will it look down on this side and on that, and not on one side only, as it is with this Gard of theirs.

Therewith he brought Ywain to the gate and so out of the city; and he turned about and showed him that on this side the face of the Great Gard was as it were blind, and in

no way looked upon the sea. And Ywain was
astonished thereat, for the place was passing
beautiful, with a broad way beneath the wall,
and a border of great trees, and between the
trees the wide water, coloured diversely with
green and purple colours. Then he looked
out as far as eye might see, and as he looked
he forgot Hubert and remembered Aithne,
for he longed greatly to know what was
the thing which she had perceived and
he not.

Then he turned back in his thought to
Hubert, and asked of him, What place is
this, and for what reason so forsaken? And
Hubert answered, Well is it that you ask
this of me and of none other. For the place
is called the High Steep of Paladore, and it
is not forsaken but forbidden: for in Paladore
the sea is held for a dread thing and an evil,
and the great ones and those of the Tower
and those of the Prince's household will have
it neither in sight nor in hearing, so that it
is not so much as named with us, save now

and then with women, or else with harpers and rhymers and the like.

Then Ywain said, Without doubt you make mirth of me, for I perceive that you are speaking one thing and thinking of another, as men use in jesting. But Hubert said, There is no mirth in the matter, save it be the mirth that covers aching bones. For at times we have sight from hence of that which in all the world we most desire, and well - begone is he that sees it: yet for this desire are we shamed and slighted, as children are hushed that speak foolishly among their elders.

But what see you, said Ywain, or what desire you to see? And therewith his heart began to go to and fro, for he knew that he was near his lady's secret. Then Hubert laughed a little and made as though he would answer him: but he answered him as it were slant - wise, for he said, Their shame is a toothless dog; and again he said, They see but little that never see Aladore.

Then of a sudden he changed his manner

of speaking, and went laughing and talking
at great random : whereby Ywain perceived
that he had done with that matter, and
would have no more of it, until he should
return into his former mind. So Ywain took
counsel with himself to lay wait for him
there, seeing that it behoved him greatly,
for his lady's sake, to hear tell of Aladore.

Then they two left the way under the
wall, and passed out between the trees : and
they cast themselves down upon the grass
and lay there for a space looking towards
the sea. And below them where they lay
was the high steep, grey and green : and
below the steep was a beach upon the
margent of the water. And as for the
water, that was of two kinds, for nigh land
it was unvexed and still, as a deep river is
still : but a mile out it was broken and
foam - flocked, as it were a great green
meadow and a thousand of white sheep
thereon, and so continued as far out as eye
could see. And Ywain marvelled to see the

breaking of the water, for there was no wind
and the tide was well nigh silent upon the
strand. And Hubert told him that it was
no marvel, for the water inshore was deep,
so that a ship might go thereon: but out
yonder, he said, no man may sail and keep
his life, for the sea is full on every side with
banks of sand, and the name of them is
called the Shepherdine Sands, and many a
one have they covered from all sight and
seeking.

Then said Ywain, They are well named
by the name of the Shepherdine Sands, for
I see the sheep plainly; but tell me this,
for what sake any man should go among
them to peril of death? And Hubert said,
For the sake of Aladore. Then Ywain
thought to anger him that he might be the
more certainly answered: so he spoke scornfully and said, What manner of men are
they that for such a sake will go to peril
of death? But Hubert was no whit angered,
and he said joyfully, Well worth the peril

and the death; for they tell such tales of
Aladore that if but the half of them be true,
then may it well be the land of every man's
desire. And this you believe not yet, for
you have not seen it, nor can I tell you
on what day or by what enchantment you
may come to see it: for a man may watch
half his life in vain, and suddenly in the
lifting of his eyes it will be there, between
sky and sea, as clear as stone in sunlight.

Then, when he heard this, Ywain was
silent for a space, and continued looking
out to seaward: but he saw there nothing
that was new, for he saw only the still
water anear him, and afar off the blue
border of the sky; and between them he
saw that pasture perilous of the Shepherdine
Sands.

CHAPTER XVIII.

OF PALADORE AND OF THE PRINCES
THEREOF.

RIGHT so came the sound of trumpets from
within the battlements: and Hubert started
up upon his feet and said joyfully how it
was the trumpets in the Great Gard blowing
to hall. And he made Ywain also to rise
up and go with him: and he brought him
again through the gate and into the city,
and so to his own lodging, and there Hubert
would have Ywain to dine with him and
with certain others. And of those others
one was named Maurice and another Bartholomy and the third Dennis, and they
were all the three of them young men and
restless in their speech as was Hubert him-

self. So they five talked together all the time of dinner, and afterward they rose not from the table but continued talking.

And as reason was, so it happened in their talk, that there was ever one that made question and four that answered: whereby at the last it seemed to Ywain that his head span round, for they four smote him with strange sayings on this side and on that, as boys will smite a top and spin it. And when they had told him the customs of Paladore concerning war and witchcraft and marriage, then they told him of the clergy and the Court. And of clergy they said that there was scarce one to be seen in all the city, for the great ones believed them not and the commons loved them not: therefore they banished them for the most part, yet not far off, lest evil should come thereby, or some sudden need. But the Archbishop they kept still within the city, for he was of the company of the Tower, or at the least so they thought of him. And of churches they made no account, but left them there: yet for the hope of Paradise there were many that went pilgrimage.

Then they all praised the Prince some deal, but of the Court they told Ywain such things as men will tell of Courts, and in part he believed them and in part he believed them not: for in his time he also had told the like and found it otherwise. But this much he heard of Maurice and took it for truth, namely that by old custom none could be Prince in Paladore save that he were a giant of his stature and of his lineage: also must no Prince take a wife save that she likewise came of giants, to the end that the same estate and goodliness might remain unto their children's children. And by this counsel, said Maurice, it came to pass that being no more of one kind with smaller folk, he that was Prince could not have ado with his people, neither in battle nor in love: but he had of them great reverence, for all men praised the doing of his lineage in time past. Moreover upon high days there would go lords before him, bearing a great sword and a crown of tourney: and when they of Paladore saw the Prince accompanied therewith, there was then no renown that they would not believe of him.

So said Maurice, and Bartholomy laughed and said further, It is true enough, yet this also is true, that our Prince is no free man, but lives in durance all his life-days. For by no old custom, but belike by fear of his greatness, it is forbidden that he come abroad into the city without he be guarded by armed guards, lest perchance he should some time break forth and go his own ways. Moreover it is provided that in his own house also, and whether he be eating or drinking or what else doing, he shall in any case be bound with chains: and in the making of such chains they of Paladore have great skill, for they will tie a man hand and foot with bonds of no seeming substance, and yet past breaking of any, save he be strongly holpen of friends.

Then Dennis laughed also, and he said
Nay, but this one thing you have forgotten,
how that our Princes have leave for all manner of hunting and fowling: and they go
freely into all such forests as are large
enough, and strike all such game as shall
come near enough. For though they ride
not with hounds, lest their horses fall down
under so great weight, yet will they stand in
covert the day long with marvellous endurance, to shoot at such few birds and beasts
as may be driven forth to them. And this
is well done, for in Paladore good hunting
brings good will, and the Prince thereby has
the love of all his people. And their love
fails not, but increases continually: for they
hold this Prince that now is, to be better
than his father, and he also was better, as
it is reported, than any that was before him:
and certainly in the old time they killed not
their game so easily, nor one fourth part of
the number thereof.

Then said Ywain, I perceive plainly that

this is a good Prince, but I am yet to seek
wherefore he should desire my presence. And
Hubert and Maurice and Bartholomy and
Dennis when they heard Ywain say so, they
were astonished, for they knew not of the
sending of Sir Rainald; and they ceased from
their laughing as men cast suddenly into fear.
And Hubert said, This is of the Tower, for I
know their handiwork of old. Then Ywain
said merrily, By seeming I also am a beast
of the game. But they four laughed no more,
and Ywain perceived that there was no merri-
ness left in them: for they dreaded the favour
of the Tower, whereby they might lose their
man as soon as they had gained him. And
in no long while after Ywain took his leave
of them: and he hastened and came to Sir
Rainald, for it was time.

CHAPTER XIX.

HOW YWAIN SPOKE WITH THE PRINCE OF PALADORE AND HOW HE TOOK UPON HIM THREE ADVENTURES.

So when he had met with Sir Rainald, they two went up together into the Great Gard: and when they came therein Ywain perceived that Maurice had told him truth, for the house was high and wide and full of great chambers, and in no way fit to be the dwelling of a man, save he were of a bigness beyond all other. Also he saw that the farther from the gate the taller were all those on whom he came: and it seemed to him as though he also took some change thereby. For when he had been brought into the chamber that lay before the chamber where the Prince was, then he began to doubt of his own stature, and his bones became shrunken and his sinews weak within him.

Then came lords unto Ywain and unto Sir Rainald, and put robes upon them and so led them in. And when they were come in they found the Prince at play, sitting upon the floor of the chamber: and beside him upon the floor were a multitude of toys, fashioned after the likeness of men-at-arms, and he made them go hither and thither as he would, so that it was a marvel to behold. And when he saw Ywain and Sir Rainald he ceased not from his playing, but he called to them lightly to come on, and take their share in his pastime. And Ywain wondered and looked hard at him: for the words were the words of a child, but he that spoke them was by all seeming a man of forty year.

Then at the last, when he had done with his playing, the Prince came to his feet, and he was nothing terrible, for all his bigness. Neither was he a child, no, not by some deal:

for he asked such questions as they ask that have seen the manner of men, and of women also. But he said not many things of his own, nor new things in any sort: and it was plain to see that his bonds wearied him. And Ywain also they wearied, for he could not choose but watch them glittering upon the Prince, so that he seemed to bear the burden of them himself.

Then the Prince brought him to a window that looked upon the city, and he asked Ywain whether it were in his mind to stay in Paladore or to go from thence shortly. Then Ywain remembered his lady Aithne, and he answered quickly that if it pleased the Prince he was minded to stay. And the Prince was pleased thereat, and he said that he looked for Ywain to take upon him certain adventures; for so did all those that had so much of skill and fortune. And Ywain answered yea, for he loved this Prince and thought no evil of him: but he knew not of what adventures he would speak.

Then the Prince looked at him pleasantly:
and he considered a little, as a man considers
of divers meats upon the board, every one of
them sweet to his tooth. Then he named to
Ywain three several adventures, that he would
have him take upon himself: and he named
the first thereof the adventure of the Chess,
and the second the adventure of the Howling
Beast, and the third he named the adventure
of the Castle of Maidens.

Then it seemed to Ywain as though his
stature had returned to him, and he answered
lightly that he would take upon him these
adventures, and that forthwith: and the Prince
gave him leave to depart, and said how that
he had done well and should yet do better.
And this also was Ywain's thought within
himself: but in the same moment he looked
upon the face of Sir Rainald, and he saw it
as the face of a fox, well pleased with the
cunning that he has practised.

CHAPTER XX.

OF THE ADVENTURE OF THE CHESS, AND BY
WHAT MEANS YWAIN BROUGHT HIS MEN
INTO OBEDIENCE.

So within a while came letters to Ywain
appointing him a day for the adventure of
the Chess. And on the day appointed he
looked forth from his house and saw how
there stood before the door a company of
great ones, and they called to him courteously
and showed him a horse that was made ready
for him. And when he came out to them they
let cover him with a cloak of silver and blue,
and they gave him for his head a cap of silver
with a plume of blue, and he perceived that
his horse was furnished in the like colours.
Then they brought him to the gate of the

city that looked toward the South, and one of them told him by what way he should go, and how it behoved him to come before noon to the Castle of the Chess, and so prove the adventure. Also another of them cast a baldrick and a horn about his neck, and said how that without doubt it should fortune to him as he should deserve, and if so be that he achieved the adventure then when he came again he should come blowing upon the horn, that his friends might make ready betimes to meet him. And some there were that laughed thereat, and among their faces Ywain saw the face of Sir Rainald.

Then he set forth, and he rode at an easy pace, for the morning was yet hoar with the dew of night and the gossamer upon the grass. And when he had passed over the high land that was before the city he came to a river and forded it, and so took the forest and went by a green road therein. And before noon he was aware of a castle that stood above the forest, and he entered in at the gate of it and came to the hall and alighted down from off his horse. And he marvelled at the manner of the castle, for he found none there to stay or to speed him, neither in the gatehouse neither within guard: yet was the hall well kept and furnished, with meat and drink on table and new rushes thereunder. Also there was a great bell above that sounded to dinner without hand or rope: so that it was easy to perceive that the place was enchanted by sorcery.

Now when Ywain had well dined he fell into a study, not knowing what more he was to do. And as he studied he heard a noise without the hall, but of what the noise might be he could not tell, for it was faint as wind or water. So he arose and went into a bay window that was beside the high table, and there was a great lattice there which stood wide open, and he came to it and looked out. And he saw there a courtyard that lay beneath the window, and the floor of it was chequy sable and white after the fashion of the tables of chess, whereby he knew that he was come to his adventure. And thereby also he perceived the meaning of the noise that he heard: for even as he looked there came out of a cloister two companies apparelled after the fashion of the chess, as it were pawns and bishops and the like, on this side and on the other. And they of the other side were all in cloth of gold with red bordures, but they of the side that was Ywain's were all in cloth of silver with bordures of blue, and of the rustling of the cloth of gold and of silver came that noise aforesaid, and other noise was there none, but that only, and the sound of it was like the whispering of the wind in an ambush.

Then Ywain looked to see who was he that should play with him: and he saw how that beyond the chequer there was a window opened, over against the window wherein he stood. And in that window was a shadow, and in the shadow a semblance like to the semblance of a man : but between the windows came the sunlight broad upon the chequer, and for the glare of it he had no certainty of that which was within the shadow.

Then he saw that the two companies were all in order arrayed upon the chequer, and the game awaiting for him: and he thought how he would send his pawn forward according to the usage, but he spoke no word as yet, for he had no desire to hear his own voice in that place. Nevertheless the pawn moved as he would have it, and immediately a pawn of the gold moved also to meet him: whereby Ywain perceived that the manner of the game was not by speaking but by thinking, and when he thought again to command a piece, then that piece also moved according to his thought.

Thus began the playing upon this side and upon that: and in the beginning Ywain had the advantage, and he looked presently to have the mastery. But the way thereto was long and tangled, and the end fell suddenly into doubt. For when the time of the stroke was come Ywain perceived that either his remembrance had failed him in strange wise, or else that he had been undone by a knight of his: for whereas by his intention the knight should have been upon the sable, now he was found upon the white, and so out of distance for the stroke. Then was Ywain in great peril, but he fought warily to recover his game, and rebutted stoutly and so came again into good hope.

But with the misadventure and the doubt, and with the slowness of the playing, the day was wellnigh passed over, and the shadow of the battlements crept softly upon the chequer. Then the sun fell more quickly to the high tower of the castle, and was gone behind it suddenly, and a little wind stirred in the coldness of his going. And Ywain saw how the wind caught the gold and silver pieces as it were in a whirlpool, and it carried them away under the cloister wherefrom they had issued: and they went after the manner of dead leaves, rustling and eddying by no

motion of their own. And he marvelled
greatly thereat, for he had supposed them to
be men like himself, but now he doubted.

Then he went to sup and to sleep, and
found all things made ready as before, but
the silence of the place choked him and the
solitariness lay deathwardly upon his spirit.
Yet he remembered how he had that day
been near to win his game, and he thought
well to amend it on the morrow and give
mate before the time of sunset. But therein
his hope deceived him, for again on the morrow his fortune was at odds with his force,
and when he came to make his stroke he
was undone by the transgression of his men:
so that his battle was disordered until sunset
and the wind right welcome to break off the
game.

And when he thought thereon, despair came
upon him, because he saw that the obedience
of his company was not as the obedience of
those others. And when he came to his bed
he lay long waking, and he cast every way

for counsel how he might make his thought to prevail more perfectly. Then in the last hour of the night he rose up out of his bed and came softly down into the cloister to see the truth of the companies, for his mind was so busy that he could not sleep. And when he was come down the day was breaking, and he found the men all together, the gold with the silver, and they lay this way and that upon the stones of the cloister, even as the wind had drifted them: and by seeming they were light and hollow, like the barren mast beneath a beech-tree.

Then Ywain stood looking upon them, and as he looked the sun rose and he saw a marvel: for with the sun rising their life came again into them, and they began to breathe and stir as men breathe and stir in their sleeping. Then he put forth his hand and touched one and another of them: and when he had touched them all, he perceived that they of the gold party were every one ruddy and warm of flesh, but they of the silver were

all white and cold as mushrooms. And in
the same instant he knew the truth of their
disobedience: for he said within himself, They
fight in my quarrel, but the heat of my blood
they lack.

Right so he knew what he must do: and
he took the hermit's knife that was about his
neck, and loosed it from the sheath, and with
the point of it he pierced his breast strongly,
so that the blood came forth in good plenty,
and the pain drew at the roots of his heart.
And he came again to them of the silver
company and with his own blood he touched
them upon the lips, until he had be-bled them
all: but the gold ones he touched not, for
there was no need. And last of all he touched
the Queen, and she awoke and rose up and
looked upon him as with remembrance: and
she put forth her hand in turn and touched
him upon the breast, and immediately the
pain ceased and the blood was stayed. And
Ywain's heart trembled as she looked at him:
for beneath her looks he saw his lady's image,

as men see faces in the fire. But she let close her eyes again and turned her from him and so fell suddenly to her sleep.

Then Ywain entered into great meditation and continued long therein, so that he walked in meditation and ate and drank the same to his dinner and came unawares to the hour of the adventure. But when the pieces were now arrayed and by his thought he began to move them upon the chequer, then he perceived that on this day the game was in his hand: for his men obeyed him with so brisk obedience that he saw them moving before ever he knew that his will was set. Also they went no more from his intent, but kept his ordinance and came all together to the stroke: whereby the gold company were discomfited and their king was both checked and mated.

Then upon the instant came a wind and thunder and lightning, and Ywain's eyes dazzled therewith. And when he opened his eyes again the castle was gone from him utterly, with the windows and the courtyard and the chequer: and he stood in a place of rocks upon a green mound of the forest. And there also he saw his horse beside him saddled and bridled, and upon the saddle bow two crowns, a gold and a silver. And he took the crowns and rode lightly towards the city: and when they of Paladore heard his horn they came forth to meet him, as they had said. Nevertheless the most of them were astonished and some displeased: for they looked not to have seen him again. And the gold crown they took for the Prince, as reason was: but with the silver crown they crowned Ywain and so brought him cityward. And as they went he fell aweary: and the sun set, and the night rose on Paladore.

CHAPTER XXI.

OF THE ADVENTURE OF THE CASTLE OF MAIDENS AND HOW YWAIN WAS COUN-SELLED TO ESCAPE THEREFROM.

Now for this adventure Ywain had great honour of all the commons, for there was no sort of fighting that they did not love, and they gave praise above measure to him that could bring men into his obedience. Wherefore they were not willing that Ywain should meet as yet with the Howling Beast, for by that adventure they had lost many that should have been great men for them. So they went clamouring that he might be assigned a day for the Castle of Maidens, for that was an adventure without pain and without peril, as the most of them deemed:

howbeit others there were that thought otherwise.

Then the Prince consented to their clamour, being counselled thereto by them of the Tower : for they looked to have Ywain either this way or that, and by favour first, if it might be so, but if not, then by foul work, as by the Beast. So on the third day they came again to Ywain with smooth faces, and they brought him forth to a great castle that was named the Castle of Maidens : and it stood a three mile from the city, in a meadow toward the sun-rising. And thither resorted all the lords of Paladore and great part of the commons, by hundreds and by thousands : and in the midst of them went Ywain with a twenty more that were of his company. And these were all young and lusty men, of lineage and wealth sufficient, and they took Ywain for their captain and banneret.

So they came to the castle anon, and found barriers thereby and lists set ready : and Ywain and his company went within the lists.

And against them there came forth as many
others, for to do battle with them: but the
custom was that they fought not with weapons
of war, but with spears of wood only. For
upon the walls of the castle were many
maidens, both young and old; and though
they might not all be young, yet were they
all too tender to look upon wounds and death.
And they were apparelled in hoods of clear
colours, right joyous and well-beseen, like
flowers arow upon the wall: and they ceased
not from making a high sweet noise among
themselves, as it were the noise of swallows
upon a ridge-tile.

Then Ywain and his were armed and came
riding merrily to tourney. And they bestirred
themselves in the best manner, so that in
one hour they had the castle yielden and
in mercy: for they that kept it fought but
for the custom's sake, and had no force to
make good their keeping. Then when he had
received the keys, Ywain entered into the
castle with all his company: and there the

maidens unarmed them and brought them to hall, that they might eat and drink and make ready to fulfil all the custom.

Now the custom of the castle was this, that whosoever should have the mastery thereof and enter as by conquest, never might he and his depart again therefrom save first they should be wedded, every man with a maiden of the castle. And they were all, both men and maids, no better than blindfold, for the manner of their wedding was by lot. And when the time for the lotting was come, the maidens sat together in a gallery, among such as were of their blood and fellowship: and they were all diversely clad in silken gear, no two alike, but every one of one only colour. Then they that had won the castle were brought in before them in coats of silk; and the coats also were diverse and no two alike, but every one of one only colour. And the colours of the maidens and of the men were such as each one pleased, according to their fantasy: and

the maidens knew not of the men, nor they
of the maidens, how they would make choice:
but when they came in presence, if any were
matched in their colours then those two were
wedded together and so departed from the
castle to their own place.

Then when Ywain heard tell of the custom
he was vexed with indignation, for he saw
how he had been snared unwitting. And he
went hither and thither, as it might be a
young wolf raging in the net: but all the
doors of the castle were barred and bolted,
so that there was no escape. Then by
chance he came upon an old dame, that was
there within a little chamber alone: and he
made excuse and would have taken his leave
of her. But she called to him and said,
Good Sir, what ails you? And he answered
her, Good Madam, what think you? Shall a
man be wedded by custom and by chance?
Then she said, So are the most of men
wedded; but if you will verily, it may
be that I shall help you therefrom. Yea,

verily, said Ywain, for I am bounden otherwhere.

Then the old dame put forth her hand
and made to give him somewhat, and when
he had handled it he perceived that it was
a silken coat, and the colour of it was of
black, both within and without. And she
said to him, Take this and abide the lotment, for it is not to be heard of among a
million of maidens that any hath chosen
black for her wedding. Then Ywain considered of her counsel, and saw that it was
good: and though it had not been good yet
he could not better it. So he made to leave
her, but first he thanked her heartily: and
that old dame looked kindly upon him, as
with remembrance. And Ywain's heart trembled within him, for he saw beneath her looks
the image of his lady, as beneath a many old
faces may be seen the beauty that was there
aforetime.

So he went from her to abide the lotment:
and as she had said, even so it was, for there

was none among the maidens that had black to her colour. Then all were matched save Ywain, and he only was left there unmatched: so that every man might see how he had taken counsel to escape. And some said that he had not wholly achieved the adventure, and others said that he had achieved it twice over, for he had prevailed both without the castle and within.

Howbeit they brought him forth with the rest that were all matched and wedded, and they came cityward with a great noise of shouting. And as they went Ywain fell aweary of them and of their customs: and the sun set and the night rose on Paladore.

CHAPTER XXII.

OF THE ADVENTURE OF THE HOWLING BEAST.

THEREAFTER Ywain continued in weariness, and in despite and anger against the great ones of Paladore: for he perceived how they had devised these adventures of a very purpose, so that they might have him at their will by fellowship or else by treason. Moreover he longed greatly to see his lady again, and could not: and of such longing also comes weariness, when a man sees time go by and nothing bettered. So Ywain made search in all Paladore, if he might but hear tell of the Lady Aithne: and he found some few that would speak of her, and little he got of them. For one would say how she was

137

gone into a far country, and one how she was ever a wanderer : and thereby they intended no good thing, for their meaning touched on Aladore, howbeit they named not the name. So Ywain went to and fro, and returned continually to the house where he had seen her : and in a three days he came there twenty times, and at last he thought to lie like a dog before her doorway.

Then at this time Sir Rainald sent a messenger to him, and said how that in two adventures Ywain had done great pleasure to his lord the Prince, and he gave him to think that by the achieving of the third adventure he might well establish himself. And Ywain believed him not, for he knew better : but by reason of his despair he made assent : for he cared not what might become of him.

So upon the morrow very early two came and called him forth : and they brought him a horse and an axe, but no gear else, and he went with them apparelled in the cloak and hat of his pilgrimage. Then he asked them of the adventure, and they told him thereof: and the manner of it was that he should enter in a certain park and hew therein a tree: and the tree might be which he would, but he must hew it within a day and a night, and it must be down before the daybreak. And as for the hazard and the pain of the adventure, they said how that came by the howling of the Beast; for at the sound of the axe it would howl beyond endurance, so that none might hear it and be the man he was aforetime.

Now the park was from the city a two hours' journey, and there was a high wall about it and a strong gate thereto: and there were some within which were appointed to keep the Beast, but they were all deaf men, and heard nothing in the world. So they that brought Ywain there unlocked the gate, and they gave him the axe and bade him enter quickly, for they were in haste to be gone. Then he left his horse and entered, and the gate was shut upon him, and he could well hear those men departing, for they rode as men in fear.

Then he looked and saw how the park was all full of thickets, very dark and tangled of old growth; and he went forward slowly, lifting high his feet. And as he went it bechanced that he struck his axe against a tree, and wounded it chipwise. And immediately there came a noise beside him like the growling of a great hound, and therewith a fear took him that was like a fear out of childhood, for it was quicker than thought and more deep within him. And he looked all ways, and saw nothing; and he listened and heard the beating of his heart.

Then he went forward again and found a place that was open ground: and it was a green valley between the thickets, and in the midst of the valley stood a goodly elm-tree. Yet was the goodliness of it by semblance only, for within bark it was long since gone and rotten. And Ywain came to the elm-tree and struck it wilfully, for he was there in a clear field and thought to see the truth of the matter. But in his stroke his senses departed from him, for there came a noise behind him such as he heard never in all his days, no, nor dreamed thereof in an evil dream. For it was like the roaring of a wild bull and like the howling of a dog upon a grave: and when he heard it his life turned black within him and his heart was angered even to madness. And he swung his axe and struck the tree haphazard, as a man may strike that is blinded in battle, and his fear was greater than his courage, and his anger was greater than his fear.

So he went smiting, and his hands were bruised and his body shaken: and the Beast howled even more loud and the rage of it pierced Ywain's heart and broke it utterly. For when he heard that sound it seemed to him that he was hated of all men and of himself also, and he felt his life perishing into dust as the grain perishes between the millstones. And his strength went from him momently, so that in no long time he had been mad or dead, save only for the help wherewith he was holpen presently.

For in his misery there came to him a sound of clear music, as a lantern comes to a child that is lost in darkness: and the music was of a reed only, yet there was within it a voice singing that was as plain as words. For as Ywain heard it he thought on old and noble wars, and he remembered in his heart the names of them which had renown therein; and he feared no more to be hated, for he had part with them. And therewith the howling of the Beast became faint and without meaning, as a noise that is very far off: and Ywain's strength came again to him and he hewed with might and with measure, and in a hundred strokes he felled the tree endlong.

Then with the fall of that tree the noise of howling ceased, and Ywain looked and saw that he had been long in his madness,

for it was now the last hour of the day. And
the music that he heard ceased not, but the
voice changed within it: for it sang no more
of old things but of new. And as he heard it
Ywain forgot all the ills that he had suffered
in all his life, and he thought on such a
place as might be the land of his desire:
and it seemed to him that he was not far
therefrom. Then his thought went from him
and he slept.

And when he awoke it was grey dawn:
and he rose up and began to go from that
place. And as he went there met him a
herd-girl with a herd of black swine, and in
her hand was a little pipe of wood, and when
Ywain saw the pipe he remembered how he
had been holpen overnight. Then he thought
to ask of the herd-girl what might be the
music which had come to him. And she held
up her pipe before him and said: Sir, there
is here no music but of this only: for here are
none but deaf men, and I that pipe to the
deaf. But whither you go there is music

enough: for you will go, as I think, by the
high-road. And therewith she left him and
went further. But as she went she looked
again at him, and she smiled as with remembrance: and in her smiling he saw his
lady the third time. Yet he saw her not to
his profit, but as a man may see an image in
a glass, which is certainly of the world
visible, but in nowise of the life thereof. So
he looked only and let her go from him.

CHAPTER XXIII.

HOW YWAIN EMPRISED TO GO TO THE CITY OF THE SAINTS AND SO INTO THE DELECTABLE ISLE.

So within a while he came to the gate, and found it wide open. And when he had passed out he looked towards Paladore, for they which brought him thence had spoken of a day and a night, and they said how they would return again thereafter, if perchance they might find him still in life and understanding. And as he looked he saw far off a company that moved upon the road hitherward: but he perceived that they came not ahorse but afoot, and they were not two but many. Also they were banded in good order as they came, and kept measure, foot by foot, and they sang all together : and that which they sang was a godly hymn, but it was some deal fierce in the singing.

Then Ywain stood still to mark their passing : but they left him not so. For when they were now going by him he saw among them the young man named Bartholomy, that was friend to him in Paladore, and Bartholomy had sight of Ywain also in the same instant. And he ceased from his singing and ran out of the company and came to Ywain and took him by the two hands : and he entreated him to be of the company and to go with them. And Ywain was little loth, for he saw how their backs were turned on Paladore, and he cared not greatly whither he went, so only he went not to that city. So he gave Bartholomy neither nay nor yea to his entreaty, but he began to go with him slowly, following behind the company.

And as they went Ywain began to ask of him to what place they were going and on

what adventure. And Bartholomy answered
him quickly and said how that it was no
adventure but a high emprise, sounding in
life and death, yea, of their very souls. For
they were aweary of Paladore and misdoubted
of all the customs there, seeing how they
were hard customs with no kindness or
godliness in them. Also he said how that in
all the world there might no peace be found,
save only in the City of the Saints : and that
was by report far off and beset of many
enemies. Yet were they vowed both to come
thither and to dwell therein, if by endurance
and good hope they might achieve their vows.

Then Ywain asked him : Whence then hath
the City this peace? And Bartholomy said :
The report of it is diverse. For some men
say of it that it cometh by one way and
some by another : as first, by conquest, for
they that dwell there do continually subdue
their enemies. But this to my thinking is
a doubtful saying. And secondly, as some
have said, it cometh by hope of reward : for

the people of the Saints trade thence into
the Delectable Isle, where a man may have
all that he will, whether of gold or ivory.
And this also, said Bartholomy, I take for
profit rather than for peace. But the third
way is by good ordinance, for in that city
they follow not their own will, nor strive
amongst themselves, but every one to serve
another: also they do nothing waywardly,
but all things by rule and governance. And
for this peace I long both by day and by
night.

Then as he heard him Ywain was kindled
a little, and he said within himself: I also
am aweary, and would serve another, and not
myself. And whether all this be true I
cannot tell, but as I guess it is an old report
that has warped in wandering. For what is
this Delectable Isle wherein a man may have
all his desire, if it be not that Aladore which
I am to look for over sea, and who knows
but I may come thither and find my lady
and my love?

But to Bartholomy he told nothing of his musing: only he took him by the arm and said that he would go with him and see this city. And therewith he pressed his arm in token of fellowship: for he drew near to him in spirit because of his voice, and because of the words which he had spoken.

CHAPTER XXIV.

HOW YWAIN SAW THE CITY OF THE SAINTS THE FIRST TIME AND HOW HE HEARD THE BELLS THEREOF.

Now was Ywain once more upon pilgrimage: yet he had not that joy which he had aforetime, when he left his house of Sulney. For then he went of his own will and followed after the boy, that was no stranger to his blood: but now he was lonely and without desire, and though he had somewhat to seek, yet his going moved rather from despair. Also the sky was changed above him, for the year began to leave summer and to turn towards winter, and the green was brown and the brown yellowing, and the nights coldened and the days drew in.

Moreover Ywain walked not so willingly with all his company: for some of them were but ale - knights which had repented them when they were adrunken, and some were swashers home from war, and others there were which loved anguishment above all, and being feeble goers would make themselves yet feebler, with peasen underfoot and hairy shirts and bodycords about them. Neither were they wholly at one in their emprise: for the half of them were in hope to be at rest in the City of the Saints, and the other half to be speedily at war against their enemies, so that many times when they sang their singing was diverse, and their fellowship most like to go agrief.

And in no long time this came to pass. For when they were a ten days gone upon their way, they that were angriest among them departed from the feeble ones: and they set off across country at great random, saying how they would take the city by assault and keep it against all others. Then they that remained went every day slower and more slow, and though they had all one weariness yet had they not all one mind. For they fell into much doubt and dispute concerning their two guides: whereof the one was a young lad that knew but little of that country, and the other was an old man and blind these many years. So at the last they were severed again into two bands and went their ways: for they that went with the youngling said how they would build a new city and forsake the old, but Ywain and a five or six more went not with them, for Bartholomy entreated Ywain against his will.

Then they set forward again, and came to a country of hills: and before they entered upon the hills the old blind fell adying that was their guide. And they found a warm village under the hills, and left him there, for it was plain to see that his time was come. Then Ywain and Bartholomy thought to go their way, to find the city or to end in seeking it; but they that had come so far would go no farther with them, for they were afeard to leave their guide, or living or dead.

So these twain entered alone upon the hills, and came through them in three days: and when they had passed through they saw the city there below them. And it lay in the midst of a plain, upon a hill that was but a great mound, with a river thereby like silver flowing: and the sea was fast by beneath the sun-setting, and the river went thereto through meadows and through boskage.

Then Ywain and Bartholomy came down towards the foothills and drew nearer to the city: and when they were upon the foothills they saw it over against them in marvellous wise. For the walls of it were of a white old age, with great bastions between all rounded, and before the walls were meadows and above them were massy trees. And within the city the roofs were of red and of grey, and among the roofs were spires

and domes and high towers innumerable: and
Ywain saw them clearly against the sky, and
they were all passing beautiful, and not one
of them like another. And there lay upon
the city an enchantment, like to a mist or
dimness upon it: for to such as stood without and looked upon it and beheld the walls
and the gardens and the high towers thereof,
to them it seemed ever to be abiding in
ancientry and peace, as of no earthly city,
but to those within it showed after another
fashion.

And while Ywain and Bartholomy stood
still looking upon the city the sun set and
dusk came round about them; and in the
dusk they saw a glimmering of lights. And
they perceived that in that city was full
plenty of chapels and of halls: for on every
side there were great windows, and in the
windows were many lights shining, rich and
orderly, window by window aline upon the
darkness. Also they heard suddenly a ringing of bells, so many and so sweet to hear,

that they were astounded with the harmony of them: for they sounded one under another, as it might be under deep and shallow water. And there was one great bell which donged below all other: and the sound of it came up to Ywain like a sound from the bottom of the sea.

CHAPTER XXV.

OF THE MANNER OF THE CITY AND HOW
YWAIN FELL ADROWSING THEREIN.

AH, said Ywain, what is this city and by whom builded? For it is certain that I came never here until now, and yet there is not one tower of it that I know not of old time. And Bartholomy answered him not, but out of the dusk a voice came and answered him, saying: Good truth and good reason, for this city was builded from the beginning, and all men are by nature free thereof; so that come they what day they will they come not as strangers but inheritors.

Then Ywain saw a man before him standing, habited after the fashion of the religious: and he saw him gladly, for he took comfort in the words that he had spoken. And

Bartholomy was comforted also, for he had
been in doubt how they should come that
night into the city, seeing that by likelihood
the gates would be shut and guarded. And
he took the man by the hand and entreated
him that he would make good his saying:
and he told him how they were of Paladore,
come hither by reason of weariness, and how
they were by name Ywain and Bartholomy.
And he answered them, Yea, but they should
have new names for a new life; for he also
had in the world a name worldly, but was
now become Vincentius, and prayed daily
against remembrance of things past.

Then Bartholomy said Ay: and Ywain
spoke no word, but his lips trembled. And
Vincent looked upon their two faces, and he
perceived the diversity of them, for he read
them as the pages of a book. And he said
to Bartholomy: What look you to find here?
And he answered Peace: and Vincent said
to him, It is well. Then he asked of Ywain
also the same question: and Ywain said

openly: I am a lover and a seeker, and I
look only to love and to seek. And Vincent
answered him: It is well with you also,
since you are come hither: for you shall
love that which you desire not, and seek that
which you have never seen.

Then he led them down toward the city:
and as they went they were astonished that
he should so have met with them in the
nick of need. But Vincent said that it was
no marvel: for that every day at the time
of twilight it was his custom to come forth
out of the city and walk abroad, to the
intent that he might lead in any that were
forwandered. So they came to the gate and
passed in with him, and he brought them
through the city to a house where they
should be lodged, and they supped there
within the hour.

And while they sat at supper they spoke
of all that had fortuned to them: and Vincent
heard them and answered them comfortably,
as a Doctor will answer them which are

diseased. But of that which he said Ywain
heard not the half, by reason of the bells
which continued sounding above the city:
for the sound of them wrapt him about as
it were with softness and with sleep. And
his weariness became pleasant to him and
his thought a dream: and he desired nothing
else but to hear those bells continually both
by night and by day.

And so it fortuned to him and to Bartholomy: for this was the manner of the
city whereto they were come, and when it
was showed to them they received it to their
joy and solace. Then might you have seen
them rising lively from their beds, and going
forth under morning mist to keep the daily
ordinance: for though the city was thronged
with all manner of folk yet there was but
one and the same rule for all. And they
rang bells at the point of day, and again
when they had broken fast: and they rang
before noon and after, and at evening and at
midnight, so that they went never an hour

without ringing of bells in some part of that city. And they took all their delight therein, and when they met together, as at board or bench or whatsoever doing, then they would have their converse of bells and of the comfort they took thereby. For they supposed that the properties of bells were many and diverse: and they heard one bell for courage and another for meditation, and one for ruth and another for gladness. And the deepest they heard for fellowship, seeing that the sound of it was very great and came into every house both near and far. And in sum, the life of those which dwelt in that city was all to ring bells and to hear them, and to do no other thing: and therefrom was their sustenance and their repute.

So Ywain went daily aringing with the rest: and he lived as it were by sound alone and thought to have found peace. For his sorrow was rocked continually as a child is rocked in a cradle, and his soul was stilled as with a lullaby.

CHAPTER XXVI.

HOW YWAIN FOUND HIS LADY IN A GARDEN.

Now in this drowsihood was Ywain living
well content: and the winter passed over and
the year began to stir again from under
ground. And March came with dust and
dryness, and then came April with sweet
showers to pierce that dryness, and in the
gardens the small birds were a-pairing and
a-nesting busily. But Ywain was still assotted
upon bells, and his mind was subdued unto
the tune of them. For he forgot neither his
love nor his seeking: but when he should
have wept therefor he remembered them only
as an old and tender tale, or as a picture of
one aforetime living, but now departed where
is neither hope nor striving.

So on a day he walked alone in a garden

of the city, and heard a sweet sad peal of bells chiming, and mused pleasantly thereon. Then suddenly he came upon a lady that was standing on a sward of daisies, and she stood between two laylock bushes, a purple and a white, and gathered flowers of each. And her face was turned away from Ywain: but his blood moved at the sight of her, and he heard the bells no longer for a singing that was in his ears.

Then the lady looked down upon the flowers that she had gathered, and Ywain saw her face athwart, over her shoulder; and though her eyes were hid from him yet he saw well that she was his own lady. For he knew her by the turning of her neck, and by her hair, and by her ear that was like the hollow of a shell: and beside all these he knew her by a reason that was no reason but certainty. And he spoke to her by her name: and she turned her about and looked at him. And he said no more, for he was astonished dumbly, like a man awakened out of sleep.

And she said to him: Tell me somewhat
of your amazement: for what came you
hither seeking, if it were not that which
you have found? Then he stood before her
stockishly, like a thing of wood: but in his
heart he went out of himself and kneeled
upon his knees before her. And he said:
Forgive me, for I thought to find you, but
not here. And as he spoke there came into
his mind the remembrance of the Queen of
Chess, and of that old dame among the
Maidens, and of the herd-girl in the wood
of Howling: and when he saw his lady here
also and in her proper shape he was be-
wildered suddenly. And he looked at her as
at one that was past his understanding, and
he cried out as in fear: What are you
verily?

But she looked at him kindly, and her
voice came to him as from a far distance,
and she said: How shall I tell you that which
I know not, seeing that I have been many
things in many times? And he looked at

her again and saw her strangely, as a man
may see his own home by moonlight: and
he cried out: Ah! lady mine and not mine!
For as I think, you were a rose in Eden,
and a golden child in Babylon, and a rain-
bow in Arcady, and a moonlight shadow on
the walls of Troy: and you were loved of
Tristram and of Troilus, and for you Lancelot
fought and Sigurd rode the fire, and the
sons of Usnach died.

And when he had so said her voice came
nearer to him, and she spoke yet more
kindly, and she said: Yet for all this I
am your lady and your earthly friend, and
I have chosen you to my servant and my
fellow-pilgrim. Then she smiled and said
further: But there is no pilgrim that can
live by sound alone, no, nor by ordinance
of others.

Then he said quickly: Must I forswear all
bells for ever? And she answered him: Not
so, but I shall show you reason. And she put
forth her hand and showed him the flowers

which she had gathered. And she showed
him first the purple, and she asked him:
How name you this, and of what colour?
And he said: It is laylock, and the colour is
the colour of laylock. Then she showed him
the white and asked him again the same
question. And he said: This also is laylock, but the colour of it is white. Then
she looked gladly at him and a little mock-
ing, and she said: You have well named
them both. And in like manner the life of
men is of the colour of life, but the life in
this city is white, and though it be life
after a sort, and sweet enough, yet is it
no life for a man. And if it please you,
we will take counsel together to depart from
it: for we must still be going if we are to
achieve our pilgrimage. But the time is not
yet: for I come and go whither and whence
I will, but you are bell-bound until the
moon shall change.

CHAPTER XXVII.

HOW YWAIN WAS BIDDEN TO AN ABBEY AND SO TO BE ENTRAPPED BY TREASON.

WHEN Aithne had so said she stood looking upon Ywain: and her face was troubled, and her soul looked out of her eyes patiently, as it were one waiting for the dawn. For she was but newly come from Aladore, and she remembered as of yesterday how her mother had spoken with her before her death. And of Ywain she knew well that he was in good truth her friend and her lover: but for the rest she doubted, and in especial whether he were of one kind with her, that they might dwell together and find no division. And Ywain looked upon Aithne, and he also was troubled, but after another fashion:

for he doubted not of her, but of himself.

So they stood looking, on the one part and on the other: and they knew not how for all their doubting their spirits were already handfast, and devising of fellowship together. Nor they knew not what was being contrived against them and against their pilgrimage. For they talked, as they supposed, in secret: but in secret also they were betrayed.

Then suddenly there came a little noise of rustling, as of one that went by stealth among the laylock bushes. And Ywain started and strode forth and looked along the garden: and he saw a man going hard away from him, and no other near that place. Then he would have followed after him: but the going of that man was marvellous, for he went not by leaping but by creeping, like a lizard going among grass. So Ywain came again to Aithne, and told her of that which he had seen: and they laughed thereat to-

gether. And Ywain was a little shamed, and
thought no more of it: but Aithne laid it by,
for she perceived that there was treason.

Then they went out from the garden, and
so departed slowly each from other: and
they made promise to come together day by
day until the third day thereafter. For on
the third day at night was the time of the
moon's changing, when they should escape
out of the City of the Saints. But when
Ywain thought thereon he could not tell how
it might be compassed. And he doubted not
without reason, seeing that he was still in
subjection. For when he was together with
Aithne he heard only her voice and nothing
else: but when he was gone from her, then
perforce he would follow the usage of the
city and hear bells to his pleasure.

Now on the morning of the third day,
when Ywain was not yet gone forth, there
came in Bartholomy to speak with him.
And he bade Ywain to a bell-ringing in a
certain Abbey of the city: for he showed

him how it was that night the festival of the Golden Bell. And he said how that bell was rung but once in the year, upon a solemn watch-night: and men were bidden thereto by no common favour. Then Ywain answered Bartholomy gladly, and was accorded to go with him. Then in the same moment he remembered Aithne and the words which she had spoken: for this was the night when the moon should change. And he would have made excuse to forsake the festival: but Bartholomy held him strongly thereto. So Ywain left him alone and went to seek his lady.

And when he had met with her, he told her all: and she said to him: This is the treason, for he that devised it is the same which heard me say how you were bell-bound. And the snare is the festival, and Bartholomy is the decoy: but he that sent him to you is some greater one, for it is he that has bidden you both. Then Ywain said: It is Vincent, for he brought us in hither,

and he crept upon us so in the beginning,
as a cat creeps upon young birds at the
dusk. And it will be hard for me to escape
from him, for he is of great power in the
city.

But Aithne smiled a little and said: A
great power and a strong magic: yet it may
be that there is a stronger. And the trial
shall be between him and me: for before
the moon changes I shall be gone into the
Lost Lands of the South. And I bid you
to my tryst as he hath bidden you to his.

CHAPTER XXVIII.

HOW THE MOON CHANGED, AND HOW YWAIN BROKE FORTH FROM THE CITY OF THE SAINTS.

So when the evening was come Ywain and Bartholomy accompanied together; and they went through the city darkling, for the moon was now in umbrage. And when they came to the Abbey where was the Golden Bell, they found a crowd gathered thereabout, and the gate well guarded: and within the gate was Vincent with certain others. And there was a great lanthorn above, and when they came beneath the light of the lanthorn Vincent saw them who they were: and he greeted them and brought them to the Chapel.

Now the manner of the chapel was this:
and it was by repute as proper a chapel as
any in that city. For it was thrice as long
as wide, and the roof was of white stone,
high embowed and carven with spreading
ribs. And the walls were of white stone
also, but overlaid below with cedar wood:
and the wood was ancient and empanelled
with many rich devices. And upon the walls
were canopies with carven tracery above, and
stalls of dignity thereunder: and below the
stalls were other stalls and again other, so
that there were of them three several rows on
this side and on that. And they which sat
therein were set over against each other:
and beside every man in every stall there
was a fair white candle burning. And with
the light of those candles the whole place
was lit and glorified: yet there was a darkness also within it, for the cedar work was
wellnigh black with ancientry. Also the floor
was of marble, lozengy black and white, and
in the candle-shine it glimmered sombrely.

So they came within the chapel, and
Vincent showed them where they should be
seated. And to Bartholomy he showed a
seat among the lowest, but Ywain he set in
a high stall beneath a canopy, among those
which were great ones in the Abbey and in
the city. And when he was come to his
place Ywain looked adown the chapel, and
he saw how Vincent had bestowed himself:
for he was set fast by the doorway, on the
one side of it, and on the other side was
set the Lord Abbot in his state.

Then when all men were in place the doors
were closed, both the outer and the inner,
and the Lord Abbot gave command and the
Golden Bell began to ring. And at the
sound of that bell the hearts of all that
heard it were comforted exceedingly, and
they folded their hands to rest: for that
which they heard was as a sweetness poured
out upon all things, whereby the wrongs of
men were hidden and their crying drowned.
And Ywain also forgot in that instant all the

ills that he had suffered in all his life: and of
the morrow he dreamed without desire. For
the fights wherein he had made forfeit and
the hopes which he had never achieved, he
remembered them but with tenderness, as
shames and perils of childhood, nothing
great: and in likewise he thought carelessly
on all that was to come. And he knew
not how long he sat there musing: for the
blood lulled idly in his pulse as the sea
water lulls before the turning of the tide.

Then upon a sudden his eyes opened and
he beheld a marvel. For over against him
there came upon the air the semblance of a
man's hand: and the hand was great and
black, and habited in a manch of black.
And it came slowly along the chapel, by no
motion that might be perceived: and as it
came the lights perished dead before it by
stall and by stall. And the lowest row were
those which perished first, and then those
next above them: and last of all the lights
that were before the canopies.

And Ywain knew not what had befallen him, for he felt in his heart a lifting of heaviness: and he looked about to see his fellows, and when he saw them he was astonished. For they started up stiffly and yet they moved not: but they sat every one in his place with his eyes staring and his mouth misshapen. And the hand went towards Vincent and towards the Lord Abbot: and their lights also perished, and the bell clanked brokenly and fell to silence.

Then came upon Ywain both memory and understanding: and joy leapt from within him fiercely, as the tide leaps beneath the wind. And he rose up and made to go forth, and they that were near him clung about him and entreated him, for they were in terror of darkness. And he tossed them from him and came striding to the door: and Vincent cried out that all should stay him. But Ywain said: Let be, your light is out: and he smote him endlong and went on and left him lying. And he came forth to the gate and burst it, and the crowd stood without wondering. And Ywain saw them as a city of sluggards and slumberers, dead before their time: and he cried, The Moon is changed, and he went through them as the wind will go through standing corn. And by what way he knew not he came to what gate he recked not: and he smote the porter with his own keys and went forth shouting into the darkness.

CHAPTER XXIX.

HOW YWAIN CAME INTO THE LOST LANDS OF THE SOUTH, AND OF THREE SIGNS WHEREBY THAT COUNTRY MIGHT BE KNOWN.

Now Ywain had in his going but one only intent, and that was by reason of his lady's word that he should find her in the South. So he ceased from his running and his shouting, and he looked upon the stars; and under the Herdsman he found the South and made to go thitherward. But he went not by the way of the high-road: for he supposed that Vincent and his would raise hue and cry after him. So he left the road and climbed forthright upon the foothills that were hard by the city. And as he had supposed, so he saw it come about upon the road beneath him: for there issued suddenly out of the gateway both lanthorns and torches, like a scattering of sparks out of a chimney. And they which bore them ran hither and thither both up and down the road, bawling and babbling in the worst manner: for their voices were harsh to hear, and out of all tune of bells. And Ywain sat above and beheld them unaware: and all their fury was by reason only that one had forsaken their ordinance.

Then he left them to their hunting, and climbed further above the foothills: and he went all night to the Southward by starlight only. And when the cold of dawn was past then the sun shone warmly upon him: and a shepherd gave him milk and bread to break fast, and he lay long thereafter in a hollow of the hills. And about him was much blossom of wild flowers, and upon the blossom came a million of bees, some great and some small, and every one of them droning busily upon his bagpipes: and also below that place was a meadow of sheep with many lambs bleating.

And Ywain had joy of those beasts and of
their droning and their bleating: for whether
he slept or wakened the sound of them was in
his ears and in his blood.

Then at the dusk he set forth again, and so
he went nine nights and days: for always he
voyaged by night and slept by day, because of
espial. But on the ninth night he came into
the lands which Aithne named to him, for she
named them the Lost Lands of the South;
and when he was come therein he knew them
by a sign, and the sign whereby he knew them
was the third of three.

For when he first came into those lands it
was evening, and not long past moonrise: and
notwithstanding that all day he had taken joy
of the sun and of the noise of beasts and birds,
yet now he had no less joy of the coolness and
the silence. And he strode forward upon the
shoulders of the hills, going swiftly and
strongly: for the moon was now waxing fast,
and the light of her lightened the green spaces
of the grass.

Then as he went his eyes also were light-

ened, and he saw the world anew. For he
perceived how that the beauty of it was of no
fading excellence, but only by long time forgotten: and belike remembered again and
again forgotten many times, according as men
made clean their hearts or darkened them.
And he saw that land as a land of gods and
not of men only: and though he saw not the
gods nor heard them, yet he perceived plainly
both their radiance and their breathing.

Then in his joy he gave thanks to the Moon,
as to the Queen of Heaven: for he knew no
longer what he did. And immediately he saw
before him an upland all hoar in moonlight:
for upon the sides of it there was a semblance
as of mist rising. Yet was that semblance no
mist, for it moved swiftly without wind: and
Ywain looked again and saw it as a company
of maidens dancing together. And their attire
was all of cloudy silk, and their feet were
bright as with ten thousand dew drops: and
their hair was whirled about them like wisps
of smoke. And it seemed to Ywain that they

danced so lightly as no thing living, save music only : for that will dance lightly without sound in the imagination of the heart.

And Ywain knew not the dancers nor how they might be named : but I suppose that they were of the hill maidens, which were of old time called by the name of Oreads. And it is like enough that they which he saw were the same : for their beauty also was of the earth but nowise transitory. And Ywain beheld their dancing gladly and kept no count of time; for as he stood the Moon passed over him and went Southing, and he marked her not. But at the last they danced more quickly, and with the sight of them his blood began to work : and he endured it not long, but he went running towards the upland. And as he ran the maidens whirled them thrice into the air, and so sank down : and Ywain saw them no more, for the earth received them, and the hill lay bare before him.

Then he took his way Southward and

looked again upon the moon : and the silver
of her beam was faded, and the sable of her
shadows, for she was well-nigh drowned in
dawn. And when the day was risen he began
to go more wearily : for in those lands the
sun was nearer and bore hard upon the wayfarers. And within a fair mile he saw a wood
before him : and the wood was full of great
ilex - trees, with laurels shining about the
margent of it. And he devised to go therein,
by reason of the shade and coolness.

But when he was come thither he clean
forgot his weariness : and he perceived that
the wood was no lonely place but full of
magic. For when he looked he saw nothing
stirring : but when he looked not then always
he perceived a stirring or a flitting or a vanish-
ing on the one side or on the other. And he
walked no more freely, but warily, by reason
of the eyes and ears that were about him :
yet he saw neither eyes nor ears to give him
reason.

Then at the last he came again to open

ground, and he laid him down upon the edge
of it within the shadow of the wood : and he
took his rest and thought to be there alone.
But within a while he returned into his rest-
lessness : for he heard a sighing as of a little
wind that came quickly and went past him
and so along the hillside upwards. And in
the passing of the wind he saw as it were three
damsels running swiftly one after another.
And as they ran his eyes were dazed with
the beauty of them and his wits stood still
and the whole world moved about him. And
he got him to his feet and laid his hand upon
his eyes : and when he had covered his eyes
then he remembered how he had seen those
damsels plainly. For they were tall and
slender of form and clear brown of colour :
and they were arrayed all in green and gold
like young boughs in sunlight. Also they ran
smoothly as a full river will run towards a
weir.

Then he lifted his eyes and looked again :
and he saw them and saw them not. For the

place was still and no thing moved upon it : but under the sun were three trees there before him. And the trees were by seeming three laurels windy-blown : for they leaned a little forward one after another, and their greenery went all one way, as it were streaming up the hillside. And Ywain supposed that in the dazzle of his eyes he had seen the trees and taken them for damsels : yet he looked long upon them as though perchance they were damsels indeed, and trees by semblance only. So he went forward pondering, and this time also he knew not that it was a sign which he had seen.

Then he began to leave the high hills, and he came into a little downland with downs that tumbled divers ways. And it was a bare land, but warm and rich : and in the valleys were cots with corn about them, and rivers going softly in deep meadows. And as he went he saw before him a beechen grove with seven trees therein : and the grove was lonely and clear of boskage, and it seemed to Ywain

that he had sight of children playing between the trees. So he came nearer, going slow and craftily: and he stood behind the endmost tree and looked through the grove, for it was but little. And that which he saw was passing strange to him: for the children were there before him, and the like of them he saw never in all his days. Naked they were and manlike to the middle,—in their flesh fat and in their countenance all merry babes: but below they were of another fashion, for their hams were wool-begrown and they were goat-kneed and goat-footed. Also their hair upon their heads was woolly and their ears were pointed and a-prick like little horns. And it was plain to see that they were kin to the beasts and of them well understanded: for one child held a squirrel between his hands, and the squirrel feared not, but kept his tail a-high; and one sat piping to a company of small fowls, which also sat and piped to him. But there was yet another child fast by, which vexed the piper with a barley straw: and he ceased not for his brother's frowning, but tickled him evilly amidst his ear.

Then when Ywain saw those babes and their playing his thoughts left him and forgetfulness and joy came upon him very suddenly, and his heart was delivered of a great laughter. And that laughter went rolling forth from him as smoke goes rolling from a fire of green wood, and like smoke it was renewed continually, bursting thickly forth without end. And the children heard it and ceased from their playing: yet it brought no fear upon them, neither upon the beasts that were their fellows. For the squirrel chattered and the small fowls piped more loudly, and the children also wantoned in laughter, and rolled upon the ground together: and when they came upon their feet again they spied Ywain and cried out joyously upon him, and they ran against him with their heads and blethered after the manner of kids. And when Ywain felt the butting of their heads and the busyness of their hands about him then there came before his eyes a haze of

brightness, so that he saw the world as it were golden and gleaming, and it seemed to him that he had returned into the morning of his youth.

Then with his much laughter his strength went from him, and for content he sighed and so laid him down upon the ground: and the children sat them beside him and tumbled one with another. And as they sported and tumbled together it bechanced that one of them struck Ywain with his foot: and Ywain started a little, for the kick was notable. And he perceived right well the reason: for he saw again the child's foot, how it was small and hard like the hoof of a goat. And instantly his thought quickened that before had been sleeping: and he knew the land whereto he had come. For this was the third sign, and sign past doubting: howbeit the first two were also signs and plain enough. But what he perceived not by Oreads and by Dryads, that he learned easily by Fauns: for of those he had but vision of the eyes, but with these there came also kicking of the flesh.

CHAPTER XXX.

HOW YWAIN HAD FELLOWSHIP WITH THE FAUNS.

So Ywain lay there upon the earth, and his laughter ebbed from him: and he set him to gather his wits together as a huntsman gathers his hounds that have been chasing over wide. And in part he gathered them but not all: for it seemed that some part of him was beyond calling and would not return. But of that he left thinking, and was content: and his heart was emptied of all thoughts save three only. For he had great desire of eating and of fellowship and of dancing: and the sun filled him with strength and the air quivered before his eyes, and he leaped up upon his feet.

Then he looked down between the beechen boles and saw where other two fauns came swiftly up the hill, leaping towards him with great leaps: and they were no children but goatmen grown with little beards upon their faces. And he stood still to meet with them, for he knew not what their dealing might be: but they came joyously to him and favoured him with their hands and with their looks and with their voices. And when they had greeted him they began to lead him away into the valley: and Ywain went with them gladly and the children followed after, lagging and sporting one with another.

And as they went Ywain beheld the grown fauns curiously: and he saw how one was by seeming older and one younger, as it might be two youths of eighteen year and twenty. Yet their faces were not two but one, for they were made after one and the same pattern: and they differed in no wise save in the hair of their beards. For of one the beard was soft and like the down within the rose-hips,

and of the other it was hard and like the
beards of barley. But in their lips and in
their eyes was nothing diverse, and Ywain
saw them as a man may see one only face
in two several mirrors: also their voices
chanted together tuneably, like voices of
young sheep in a flock.

And they showed Ywain how they were
called: for they pointed each at other and
so named their names, and the older one was
called Panikos and the younger one was
called Paniskos. Then Ywain spoke their
names and laughed and he showed them his
own name also: and he laughed again, for
they used it strangely, bleating somewhat in
their speech. Then in the like manner they
showed him other words, and he learned of
them easily: for they spoke of no far matters
but only of such as were according with his
appetite. And in especial they spoke of eating and of drinking and of music: and also,
as he supposed, of hunting and of sleeping.
And though Ywain knew not yet what they

would say concerning these things, yet he
knew certainly that they spoke thereof. And
he perceived their joy, and had fellowship
with them : for he saw how they lived far
off from carefulness and perplexity, and how
their life was mingled continually with the
beauty of the earth.

CHAPTER XXXI.

HOW YWAIN MET WITH A SHEPHERDESS AND HEARD A MUSIC, AND HOW HE HAD SIGHT OF ALADORE THE FIRST TIME.

THUS began Ywain to be consorted with fauns, and to live after their manner: and he slept with them that night in a little wildwood fast by a river. And before they slept they gave him to eat of such things as they had: and truly his supper was no feast. For the fauns live all by nuts and by grains, and have no bread: also they will taste flesh but they know not the use of fire. So on the morrow early they caught a good fish and tore it: and when they perceived that Ywain loved not raw meat, then they had pity on him. And they left the river and brought him to a shepherd's hut, and they made him understand that he should go nearer and knock upon the door. For they knew that where there were men, there belike would be men's meat, whether of bread or of flesh.

So Ywain came to the hut, and knocked upon the door: but he heard no voice within. And when he would have knocked again a second time he dared not: for he knew that there stood one within and listened silently. Then he devised to speak instead of to knock: and he spoke the greeting of a pilgrim, humbly. And while he was yet speaking the door was opened, and there was there a young shepherdess standing upon the threshold. And when he saw her his heart began to beat furiously: and the beating of it upon his ribs was like the galloping of a horse upon a green road. For the shepherdess stood looking at him out of youth and fearfulness: but the face was the face of his lady and of no woman else.

N   193

Then his voice changed, and he spoke again to her trembling: but she nodded with her head and answered not. And she put forth her hand to bring him in, and he perceived that it was brown and hard, and he looked again and saw how her face also was brown as with the burning of one summer upon another. Then he said within himself: My lady was never so: yet if this be not her body it is her soul, and in all her shapes I am to serve and follow her.

Then the shepherdess gave him to eat: and that which she gave him was no rich man's portion. But without doubt she changed it in the giving: for the bread was fine bread between his teeth, and the flesh was as the flesh of swans and peacocks. And while he ate she looked upon him, and he also looked upon her: and he ate but little by reason of his looking and his delight. And when she perceived this she forsook him suddenly and went out: and immediately his hunger increased upon him and he dealt shortly with all that she had given him. Then she came again suddenly, and looked upon the bare board, and laughed: but in all this time she spoke not one word, so that Ywain marvelled and was some deal discomfited.

Then he called her by her name, Aithne: but thereto she shook her head and continued saying no word. And he said to her : What do you in this place, and by what name shall I call you ? And again she answered not, but she took two shepherd's crooks that stood behind the door of the hut, and one of them she kept and one she gave into his hand, and so led him forth. And they came together to the sheepstead and untied the wattled cotes, and loosed the sheep: and together they went hillward in the cool of the morning.

Now as they went together Ywain looked about him, and he saw the fauns that were his friends: and they stood beside the valley road in a place whereto Ywain should come presently. And he called to them joyfully,

and they heard him calling: so that he hoped
they would have stayed for him. But when
he was now within a pitch of them, he saw
how they were suddenly gone away: for they
ran swiftly from him towards their wildwood,
and the reeds of the river hid them as they
ran. Yet they went not with one mind or
one fear: for one of them stayed in his running and returned. And Ywain had sight of
him among the willows, peering with bright
eyes: and he perceived that he was stealing
fast upon them, and going from tree to tree.
And when they were at the turning of the
road, where they must leave the valley and
go upon the hill, then the reeds rustled and
crackled beside the road: and the faun broke
forth suddenly upon them, and he was that
one that was the younger of the two. And
he looked no more upon Ywain but upon the
shepherdess only: and he stooped down and
took her hand and nosed in it lovingly as a
deer will nose in the hand of her that feeds
him. And Ywain spoke to him by his name:

but thereat he started up and went leaping after his fellow, and rustling like a wind among the reeds.

Then the shepherdess led Ywain forth upon the hill, and behind them was the river and before them was the little beechen grove. And they came to the grove and sat within the shade of it and looked over the valley: and the sheep went cropping the wild thyme and the milkwort, and clanking pleasantly with their bells. And the shepherdess looked downward upon Ywain, for he lay before her at her feet: and he turned and looked upward into her eyes. And as he looked the day went over him in a moment of time, between two beats of his heart: and he lacked speech of her no longer, for he dreamed under her silence as a man may dream under a starry night.

Then she rose and led him again downward: and the sheep went down before them to the river, and fell to drinking greedily. And as they drank the wind of evening came

softly down the stream, and upon it came a
sound of piping: and Ywain's heart ached
to hear that piping, for it was of a sad and
piercing sweetness. Then his feet began to
move beneath him, and he left the sheep to
their drinking and went toward the music.
And he came to a glassy pool among the
rocks: and upon the rocks was the young
faun sitting, and playing on his pipes, and
under his feet was the evening sky, shown
clearly upon the water of the pool.

And Ywain came near, for the music drew
him strongly: and he stood and looked upon
the pool, and he saw the sky therein. And
he saw it not as sky but as a great region
of the sea: for the clouds upon it were like
lands of earth, and they lay there after the
fashion of bays and heads and islands. And
there was a coast that lay fast by him, as it
were beneath his very feet: and it ran to the
right of him and to the left, and beyond it
was the void space of the sea. And as he
looked upon the coast he knew it well: for

he stood by seeming upon the High Steep of Paladore, and looked out over the Shepherdine Sands.

Then with the beauty of the place he fell to longing, and because of the music that he heard his heart was restless: and he desired greatly to be seeking for the land wherefrom that music came. And in a moment it was there before him, beyond the void space of the sea. And the form of it was as the form of Paladore, with the city and the steep all fashioned out of cloud: but it lay lonely and far out, like an island of the West. And a light was upon it more delectable than all the lights of sunset, so that it seemed to burn also in the eyes of him that saw it: and the light and the music increased together, and together they faded and ceased. And when they ceased Ywain turned him aside to weep, for he perceived that he was homeless.

But as he turned he saw his lady beside him standing, and she spoke and called him

by his name as one that knew him afresh and
was no more bedumbed. And he cast himself
into her arms and kissed her: for he knew
that he had had sight of no earthly city but
of Aladore. Then he looked again upon the
pool, if by fortune he might see that city
again: and he saw but a ripple on the water,
for with his hoof the faun had dabbled it.

CHAPTER XXXII.

HOW YWAIN LIVED AS IT HAD BEEN IN THE GOLDEN AGE AND HOW HE WAS STILL UNSATISFIED.

RIGHT so came the night and they got them homeward. And Aithne went to her hut, where she had her living among the shepherds, but Ywain returned and rested with the fauns. And he slept not, but lay a great time waking, and longing for the morrow morn : whereby he hastened it not, but delayed it rather. And this is the folly of men that they will look ever forward to that which they have not, and take no rest in that which they have. For Ywain had that day gathered to fill both his hands — namely, by seeing Aladore and by taking of his lady in arms :

and in a long life there will come but few such days, so that it were wisdom to cherish them in memory. But Ywain remembered scantly that which was past and gathered, for his mind was all on the kisses that were to come: and folly it was past gainsaying, but of such folly is the life of man.

So he lay longing, and arose in hope, and continued many days after the same gait. And his desire fled still before him, and he followed and thought not on the way of his going: for to him one day was like another, and one night was like another, and he counted them no more than a child will count the beads upon a string. But Aithne counted them and laid them by, and when she counted them she trembled. For she also would have him gone on pilgrimage, seeing that so only might she meet with her love in Aladore: but many times she said within herself: Not yet, poor lady me, for none knows what may fortune, and belike this is all that shall be mine.

Aladore

Now the manner of their days was after the manner of the Golden Days. For their meeting was in the freshness of the morning, when all things are made new: and they ate and drank together with few words, and between them was a bowl of milk, and over it they laughed one at another with their eyes. For about the bowl was a thread of scarlet wool, and Ywain knew well for what reason it was there: yet would he ask many times for asking's sake. And Aithne said how it was there of great necessity: for she set it there to be a witchknot, to draw her love to her by shepherd's magic. Then many times he broke the thread and cast it on the ground, and always when he came again the knot was freshly knotted upon the bowl. So out of nothing they made much, after the old fashion.

Then with their sheep they took the road, and came thence upon the upland pastures. And while the day was yet cool they two went wandering alone, and marvelling at all the diverse flowers upon the hills. But when the sun was overhead and the air began to tremble upon the rocks, then beneath a little cliff they found a spring of water flowing out continually and sparkling like crystal above the pebbles. And thereby grew tall fir-trees, and white poplars, and cypresses and planes, and on the branches the cicalas were chirruping, all sunburnt, and the ring-doves were moaning one to another of love. And below them were many flowers of fragrance, such as fill the meadows in the heyday of the year before it wanes: and all the land smelt sweetly of summer, and the wild bees went booming about the water springs.

And thither came Ywain to his shepherding and he forgot the world as though it had never been. For he remembered neither land nor gold, nor his old fame among men: but he sat with his love beneath a rock and held her in his arms, and they murmured one to another, and watched their sheep feeding among the thyme. And when it drew towards evening then they came downward from the hill, and listened to hear the young faun's music: for among the fauns there is not one that dare pipe at noon, but at evening they will pipe without fear. And when there was a sound of music then Ywain came always to the glassy pool, hoping that he might have sight of Aladore. And when the pool was still he saw it, for the piping of the faun was of a strong magic, beyond all understanding of him that made it, as happens many times to them that make music. But Ywain had of that magic more pain than joy: for the vision which he saw thereby was of no substantial city, but an image made in water. And to find that city in truth his heart was restless with desire, for he knew that except he came there he might have neither fulness of love, neither abiding.

CHAPTER XXXIII.

OF THE MADNESS OF THE FAUNS, AND HOW
YWAIN FORSOOK THEM SUDDENLY, AND
HIS LADY WITH HIM.

MOREOVER when midsummer was now come
Ywain began to misdoubt him of the fauns:
for from gentle they were become fierce, and
when he saw their eyes he saw them changed,
as a sky that is hot with thunder. Also they
departed from him continually, both by night
and by day, and he saw how they went wandering alone and secretly: and when they went
forth they went as it were ravening like
beasts, and when they came again they came
weary and shamed before him, as with the
shame of men, for in their nature they were
divided between two kinds.

Then upon a night it fortuned to Ywain

that his sleep was broken, because of the moonlight that crept upon him. And at the last he awoke utterly, and in the moonlight he saw the young faun beside him sleeping, but the old one he saw not, for he was plainly slunk away. And Ywain took but little heed of him, as at this time, for his own head was weary and he had yet no comfort of the night. So he turned him and lay still again and thought to sleep.

But as he lay there came a sound from far off, like the cry of one that shrieks suddenly in fear. And with that sound Ywain also was affrighted, and his heart stood still, and he held his breath to listen. And there was silence for a space, and he said: It is an evil dream, for it is long since that cry was in my ears. And therewith the cry came again, louder than before, and Ywain perceived that the voice was the voice of a woman: and he started up and leaned upon his hand, and the sweat pricked him suddenly among the roots of his hair. And the young faun also started up out of sleep and

stood before Ywain listening: and Ywain saw
his eyes that glittered under the moon, and
his mouth that grinned and trembled, as a
dog's mouth grins before he bites.

Then the crying came again the third time,
and continued more and more, and it was by
seeming nearer, as of one running and crying upon the hillside; and Ywain thought
to know the place, and he leapt upon his
feet to go thither. But when he would have
gone he could not, for the young faun cast
his arms about Ywain's knees and held him
fast. And Ywain looked down upon him and
was astonished, for aforetime he had seen
him as a thing young and tameable, and of
a nature softer than the nature of men. But
now he saw the teeth of him and heard the
growling: and therewith a red hatred came
upon Ywain, and his heart swelled up to bursting, and he fell upon the faun and beat him
with fists upon the head. But the faun loosed
him not for all that, nor ceased not from his
mirth, and they two rolled upon the ground
and fought together, the one grinning always

and the other sobbing, for Ywain wept fiercely with rage to be so hindered.

Then at the last he caught the faun and choked him, and so cast him grovelling: and he escaped out of the wildwood and began to climb upon the hill. And now that he was escaped he knew no longer whither he should go, for there was no more sound of shrieking, but a great silence of moonlight and solitude. And he went to and fro upon the hillside and found there no living thing: and at the last the sky began to lighten towards dawn, and his strength left him, so that he laid him down and slept he knew not where.

And when he awoke the sun was high, and he looked adown the hill and saw Aithne coming towards him, and she was leading forth her sheep, for it was time. And as she came he saw her loveliness while she was yet far from him, for her going was both proud and womanly, and she showed forth in it the fashion of her heart. And when he saw that he thought on pain and terror, and he had great pity upon all women, and he went quickly to meet her and said: What have we here to do, for we should be gone long since. But she looked at him and saw how he was already weary, even in the first hour of the day, and how he was troubled beyond measure, even in her presence that loved him: also she saw how he was soiled and somewhat be-bled upon the hands. And she touched his hand with her hand and asked him of his hurt, and for what cause he would be gone. And he told her no truth, for he would not tell her of his pity, but he spoke of himself only, and he said: I am afraid, for I go in peril of my life, by reason of the fauns. Then she said: Dear heart, be not afraid, for I know the fauns, that they will be cruel at their hours, and I have a spell to tame them, for they are but beasts. Yea, said he, they are my brethren of the half blood. And now I beseech you that you lay down your crook and leave your sheep to feed as may befall them, and let us begone by what way you will. And she delayed and asked him

Whither? And he said: I know not whither, but this I know, that I have fought with my kin, and I have dwelt among them long enough.

Then Aithne sighed, and she turned her about and looked upon the valley, and the sun lay broad upon it, and the morning shadows, and the river ran bright among the willows below and in the rocky pools above. And she sighed again, and then she said: It is nothing, beloved, for we have been long together, and we have that which hath been and that which shall be. But as men say, a joy that ends is never long enough, so now I sigh because I must bid this place farewell. And I knew always that we must some day be gone from it: and I waited only for your will. This is my will, said Ywain: and he cast her crook upon the ground, to be a token to them that should find it lying. Then he took her by the hand, and they looked again upon the valley: and they kissed for comfort and for memory, and turned them and went together across the hills.

CHAPTER XXXIV.

HOW YWAIN AND AITHNE WENT FLYING
BETWEEN SUN AND MOON.

THEN they went hastily until it was past noon,
and Ywain would not that they should stint,
till at last they wearied both, and lacked
strength for lack of meat. And they espied
a shepherd's hut all lonely among the hills,
and it stood fast by a thicket, and they knew
not whose it might be, for it was far off from
the valley of their dwelling. So they came
thither and found it empty, for the shepherds
were abroad with their flock. Then they went
within the hut and shut to the door and
thought to rest them awhile. But Ywain sat
him down beside the window and hid himself,
that he might keep watch, for he doubted
that they were not yet wholly escaped.

And when he had watched for the space of
half an hour he saw how that there was something stirring in the border of the thicket:
and presently came forth the young faun,
going warily upon his hands and upon his
shanks. And he cast about him on this side
and on that, nosing the earth as a hound upon
the trail: and he began to creep toward the
hut, and Ywain moved not but laid hold upon
his staff. But in the same moment he looked
beyond the faun and saw two shepherds which
came coasting the thicket, and he heard their
dogs behind them barking and driving in the
sheep. And the faun also heard them and
was discomfited: for his wits had been all
upon the trail and he was well-nigh trapped.
And the shepherds saw him and cried out
upon him and made to beat him with their
crooks, but he ran with great leaps, and
passed before them and was gone into the
thicket.

Then Ywain went out to meet the shepherds,
and to question them, for he perceived that
they were come home from pasture before

their time. And they said that they had great need to come, for that there was a gathering of fauns throughout all the country, and it was the time of their madness wherein they would be fell and beastly.

Then Ywain told his tale also, and they counselled him earnestly to go further, for they understood how that he was hated of the fauns, and belike against him was their gathering, and against none other. So Ywain brought his lady forth in spite of weariness, and the shepherds gave them such meat as they had, and sent them away.

Then Ywain began to be afeared as he had never been afeared in all his days, for he saw how his lady was fallen lame with the roughness of the hills: and this that was before him was no proper warfare, wherein a man may die reasonably, but a desperate and unclean fortune, to be overtaken by beasts in darkness. And on every wind he heard voices, and behind every tree he saw the shadow of his enemies, so that he went continually as through an ambush, forlorn of hope. But

Aladore

Aithne spoke always with good cheer, and made light of fauns, as one that had a spell to subdue all creatures at her will. And almost Ywain believed her, for she was stedfast beyond all bravery of feigning.

Then at the last the sun began to fall more swiftly to his setting, and a great perplexity came upon Ywain. For he supposed that in the darkness would be the end of all, but he knew not how nor in what point of time: and he had a longing to say somewhat to Aithne, yet for shame he could not say it, lest by chance after despair there should come deliverance. And therein his heart betrayed him not, for his fortune was better than his fear.

Thus they continued going forward, and speaking as in hope: and though they spoke deceivingly each to other, yet their spirits were in peace together. And as they went they looked upon the sky westward: and there was a little span between the sun and the sky border, and by that span they saw their life and measured it. And the sky was

clear above and without cloud, but the sun
was greatening below in a mist of rose: and
against the mist was a black jot, as it were a
black crow homing towards nightfall. And
when it came nearer they saw how it was in
bigness greater than a crow and in colour
diverse: for the light went through it and
yellowed it, and it flew more swiftly than a
bird. Also it came with a sound of humming,
like a great bee, and the nearer the louder,
till the air was shaken with the humming
of it, and the blood quickened in them that
heard it. And Ywain and Aithne stood still
to look upon it, and they saw that it was
by seeming a man which flew with wings:
and he came over them where they stood
and went about them in a circle like a
buzzard, wheeling lightly and looking down
upon them.

Then Ywain made a sign requiring succour
of him: and he took Aithne into his arms and
made to shelter her, and with his staff he
swung great strokes about him, as it were

against a host of enemies. And his sign was well understanded of him that was flying, for he dropped swiftly down upon the earth, and he put off his wings and came running where Ywain was and Aithne. And they saw how that he was a man like unto themselves, but tall and strong and comely out of measure, and at a word he perceived their peril and the evil malice of the fauns. Then hastily he did on his wings, and he took a thong, and when he had bound Ywain and Aithne with the thong he made them fast beneath his pinions, and so mounted lightly upon the air.

And Ywain and Aithne looked down and marvelled and held their breath, for the whole earth fell from them suddenly. And for a moment they had sight of fauns, running together like ants beneath them : and then they saw the fauns also fall from them and become as dust. And the sun set, and the moon rose, and they went flying swiftly between the sun and the moon.

CHAPTER XXXV.

OF THE CITY OF DŒDALA, AND HOW AN OLD DAME THEREIN DESPAIRED OF IT.

So they went swiftly and spoke no word, being astonished unto dumbness: for their life was changed suddenly and they were in no place of the world. But he that bore them held his course, and he flew Eastward by the space of an hour. Then they were aware how he sloped downwards in his flight, and they looked and saw beneath them a great city on the border of the sea, and in no long time they came lightly down and took land before a gate that was there. Then they three entered afoot into the city, and they came quickly to a good house and were received therein.

Aladore

Now the house was the house of an old and noble dame, by name Eirene, and she was the mother of Hyperenor, which had borne Ywain and Aithne upon his wings. And them she greeted courteously, and received them to be her guests while it should please them: but to her son she spoke after another sort. For in one and the same breath she dealt him sweet words and bitter, giving thanks to all the gods for his home coming, and also bidding him begone where she might never be troubled with him more. And after this manner she continued all supper - time, and she would have Aithne to know how she was the most miserable of all women living.

For I was born, she said, in a city far off from this, in a land of other men and other customs, and I came hither blindfold in my youth. And the veil wherewith I was blinded was the veil of marriage, as it fortunes to the most of us. For of this city I knew nothing, but I supposed it to be an ancient city and a pious, with gods and customs like our own:

and I found it given over to a madness of inheritance, and by special wrath of heaven accursed and punished. For this is the city of Dœdala, where is the tomb of Dœdalus, whom they call the father of inventions: and though his bones be perished, yet they keep here his impiety, and do after it. And their madness is beyond belief, for there is nothing that they will do by way of nature if by any means they can devise to do it otherwise, as by mechanemes of iron or brass. And at my first coming they were assotted upon chariots of fire, and afterwards upon a hundred other devices, full of noise and dangerous exceedingly: and now they sin with the very sin of Dœdalus. For when he had found out many inventions, he found out this also, to fly above the earth with wings: a thing plainly hateful to the gods, for if it had been their will, they would have made men like to birds in the beginning. But their will was not so, and they have sent upon this city the curse of Dœdalus: for as the god took his son from

him and cast him dead upon the sea, so now
it is with us, and heavier a hundredfold.

Then the old dame wept bitterly, that it
was pity to see, and her son ran to her and
knelt beside her and handled her lovingly.
And when he had some deal comforted her,
then he spoke merrily and said how it was
shame to lay so much on gods and to make
them unreasonable and so bring them into
judgment. And it may be, he said, that it
is we, and none other, that are the gods, for
certainly we are greater than our fathers,
and there shall yet be greater that shall
come after us. But his mother rebuked him
and said: I will not hear such words; for
your fathers kept due observance and lived
long, and you of this generation do reverence
to none, but you fly outrageously in the face
of heaven, and your youth is cast down upon
the earth as upon a dust-heap. And to what
profit? for you die like the flowers and leave
no name behind you. And Hyperenor said:
So be it, but our fruit shall follow us: for

it may be that our sons shall fly and not
fall. But Eirene wept again and said: You
are great givers, for you tear your mothers'
hearts to feed your children.

Then Aithne went to her to comfort her,
for she was sorry in her heart for that old
dame, and she saw how she had no other
son but this one only, and him she looked
daily to lose. And Ywain also had pity on
her, for there is no man that can bear to
look upon a woman weeping. But he was
divided in mind, and in part he was pitiful,
as need was, but in greater part he took
side with Hyperenor and upheld him to have
the right of it. For he saw how the young
man was a great knight and strong and
passing comely: and though his words were
some deal big, yet his voice was slow and
courteous, as the voice of one that would
make good. Also in his doctrine Ywain
upheld him: for in all wars there will be
some that die, and they die gladly to subdue
a kingdom, though for themselves they see

it not nor enter into it. But most he loved
him as one that would dare and do, and of
his daring and his doing he would willingly
hear more: for it seemed to him a great and
marvellous thing that men should fly, that
so they might come into all places of the
earth, yea, and perchance into some that
are beyond.

CHAPTER XXXVI.

OF A PROMISE THAT WAS MADE TO YWAIN, AND HOW HE TOOK WINGS TO SEEK FOR ALADORE.

THEN after supper the old dame went out, and Aithne with her, and Ywain was left there with Hyperenor, and they two sat a long time talking together. And as they talked they drank their wine, by cup and by cup: and they sat beside a window, and the window was open wide, looking upon the city and upon the lights thereof, and the night over them was blue and spangled with bright stars. And Ywain perceived how that Hyperenor was no longer strange to him, but near and kind as out of old friendship: and he spoke with him concerning many matters, and was

224

accorded with him continually. Then at the last he spoke of Aladore, and he told him how that he must of necessity come there to be wedded with his lady, and how he had sight of that land as it were of a cloud in heaven, yet he could by no manner of means attain to find it.

And Hyperenor received his saying readily, and began to make him large promises: for he was such an one that in his book was no word for things impossible. And he said how he would give Ywain wings, and learn him quickly how he should use them, so that in one day he might well come to fly with all ease, if he had but good courage and continuance of fortune. And as for Aladore, he had no knowledge thereof, but to find it he took to be no hard matter. For if such place there be, he said, be sure that flying will bring us to it, save it be at the sea bottom: and in that case, he told Ywain how that he had yet another mechaneme to do his purpose, so that by wing or by water Ywain should certainly come thither.

Then when Ywain heard those words he was fain to believe them, and he began to feel his wings uplifting him. And he doubted not of Hyperenor, but he thought to know more of his mind concerning Aladore: therefore he asked him toward what quarter of the earth they should begin their seeking. And Hyperenor answered Toward no quarter: for that the land was plainly no place of earth, but a floating isle, after the kind of the isles which float upon the sea, and belike it would be found in the region of the stars. And Ywain marvelled at his knowledge and took comfort of it: for he also believed that it was no earthly city which he sought, but what else it might be he knew not, until it was showed him reasonably.

So he heard Hyperenor and was content, and looked upward to the stars: and he beheld their aspect such as with his eyes he never yet beheld it. For he knew them of old both by stars and by constellations, but now first he saw their images in heaven: and behind every constellation was an image, like a great shadow decked with stars, and the shadows went about the high dome like servants of the gods, going silently in their appointed order. And Ywain knew no longer where he might be, for he saw no more the lights of the city nor heard the voice of Hyperenor that talked beside him; also it seemed to him that time was fallen dead, so that the world was void and still, as a glass is void when all the sands are run down upon the heap. And he awoke as from long dreaming: but he perceived that Hyperenor knew not how he had been from him all that space. So within a while they betook them to their rest.

Then on the morrow they rose up early, and came to a meadow ground which lay before the gate of the city: and Hyperenor gave Ywain wings according to his promise, and shewed him all his own skill therewith.

And Ywain received his teaching quickly, and brought it to good market, so that in no long time he went which way he would: and he wearied not nor failed of strength, but his wings upbore him lightly without labour, for they were so devised.

And when it was evening he thought to prove his adventure: for he was not willing to return into the house to Aithne until he should have somewhat to tell her. And when the sun was now going down into the sea Ywain did on his wings again, and scanned all the regions of the sky: and there was no cloud near the sun, but over against his setting there was one only cloud, made golden by the light of evening. And under the cloud was the moon rising, and she came up out of the mountains of the East and went climbing towards the cloud. Then Ywain called to Hyperenor and together they leapt into the air.

Then at the first they went wheeling about and about, to gain the height of the sky, and the dusk began to fall softly round them. And Ywain looked down in his wheeling, and there was the city of Dœdala very far beneath him, and it smallened and darkened continually, so that save for the moonlight upon the towers he had soon seen it no more. But for a time he saw it still lying cold and white by the border of the sea. Then he looked up and saw the stars, and above him Hyperenor flying beneath the starry roof: and Ywain followed him and they left their wheeling and flew straight toward the cloud above the moon. And the moon rose up to meet them, and the light of her came cold upon their faces, and they strained in their flight to hold their way above her, so that they flew faster and faster into the hollow of the night.

And as they went the coldness of the void entered into Ywain's blood, and he felt no more neither hope nor fellowship, and his love lay frozen within him as the root of a flower lies frozen in winter. But his thought was busier than aforetime, and his desire was to

know all things which might be known.
And he looked down again toward the earth,
and saw it as a thing without life or meaning:
for in bigness it was lesser than his hand,
and it fell beneath him like a stone that is
hurtled from a cliff. And he said within himself: What is that to me, for it is but one
amongst many: and he looked up again to
Hyperenor that he might follow him further.

But when he looked he saw him not nor
the cloud neither, and in a moment his
thought was dazed within him, and went
staggering like a man struck suddenly upon
his eyes. For on every side the stars were
changed about him, and they kept no more
the order of their constellations, but they
were as a crowd rushing upon him, countless
and disorderly. Then he looked again upon
the moon, and saw her as it were hard by
him, and he was yet more in dread: for she
was no living land but a bare plain and cold,
and upon the plain were hills like naked
bones, and black pits like the pits of dead

men's eyes. And in the same instant he saw
against the moonlight Hyperenor, falling like
a dead bird towards the earth. And in his
fall he came by Ywain and went fluttering
past him, and Ywain leaned over and peered
after him, and the coldness left him, and
the blood came again swiftly from his heart.
And he stooped his head and went whirling
down the gulf, and the winds rushed up to
meet him and bore him whither they would;
for his strength was as the strength of a leaf,
that falls at end of summer.

CHAPTER XXXVII.

HOW YWAIN CAME THE SECOND TIME TO THE HERMIT, AND HOW HE TOOK COUNSEL OF HIM.

Now Ywain fell swiftly earthward, and belike the time of his falling was no great space: but to him it seemed long, beyond reckoning, for his wits were battered and edgeworn, as a stone is worn by a hundred years of rolling. And whiles he dropped headlong through the void, and whiles the wind came up beneath him and lifted him lightly, so that he rose and fell as it were upon great waves of the sea. But at the last he came hurtling down upon a forest, and among the trees of it his wings were caught and broken: yet was Ywain not broken therewith, but he took the earth easily and recovered himself.

Aladore

Then he got to his feet and began to go
through the forest, and it came to his mind
that he was thrice lost, and not once only:
for he was gone from his lady and from his
friend, and he knew not where to seek them
nor in what place of the world he might
himself be wandering. And for Aithne he
prayed to see her again in no long time, for he
knew how she could come and go by her own
magic, that was her gift of faery: but for
Hyperenor he lamented without praying, for
he supposed that he was gone beyond that.
And for himself he raged against fate, for it
seemed to him that his life had fallen suddenly
from light to darkness, as a lamp that is
thrown down, and though it be not broken,
yet it cannot be kindled again, but cold it
lies and blackened that was burning but a
moment since. And when he perceived that,
then he bit and beat against time as a wild
thing will bite against the bars of a cage.

Howbeit he continued still upon his way,
and suddenly he perceived that he was in

no strange path : for he was going between
tall pines, and beyond the pines was a stream
that ran burbling, and a bank with great
beeches upon it, and he went forward quickly
as one that well knows what he shall find.
And as he thought, so it fortuned to him,
for he came by sunrise to a bare lawn under
a cliff, and in the face of the cliff was a door
carven and a window or two, and it was the
house of the hermit that was friend to him,
and right glad he was to see that place again.

And when he came there the sun was risen,
and the hermit was coming forth out of his
house in like manner as he had done aforetime, and in like manner he brought bread
and broke it for the small fowls of the forest.
And Ywain was amazed to behold his dealing :
for there had come no change upon the man,
nor upon the place, nor upon anything therein,
but Ywain only was changed within himself
and made new by time and trouble.

Then he stood still beneath a beech-tree,
and called with a quiet voice and bade the

hermit a good morning: and the hermit moved
not but answered him yet more quietly, and
continued feeding his birds. So they two
came together without ado or overmuch
heartiness, but inwardly they were quickened
both, as with memory and friendship. And
they went together to the stream, and when
they had given bread to the fishes, then they
did off their garments quickly and took the
pool as they had done aforetime: and they
sported joyfully and so came home to break
their fast together.

Now as they sat at table Ywain looked out
from the window, and he saw the sunlight
upon the lawn, and he heard the murmur of
the stream, for the sound of it came by upon a
little wind of morning; and he bethought him
how the times were changed, and all his mind
unknown to the hermit that sat beside him.
Then the hermit said to him: We are strangely
met again: for in a year this place is nowise
changed, and I have gone but a little downward on the byway of my life, but you have

journeyed far to the forward, and are come within sight of your desire. And Ywain was astonished and asked him : How know you that which has befallen me, for it is a long tale and I have not yet told a word of it. And the hermit answered : I know it not, but there is little need of telling. For I set you forth on your way to Paladore, and therein you followed your desire : and without doubt there met you by the way a woman, for by every man's way there is a woman, and without doubt you learned of her that which all women teach. And for the rest, you have encountered this and that adventure, and though you have proved them well, yet have you failed of your achievement unto this present, for there is hope in your eyes and no certainty, and you are here alone and wandering.

Then Ywain opened his heart, and he told his story by part and by parcel, until he had told it all. And when he had ended his telling the hermit was silent, and he sat there stilly

and moved no more than if he had been lost in
sleep. And at the last Ywain said to him:
That which I have done, is it well done or ill?
Then the hermit stirred a little, and sighed
deeply, and so fell again to silence. But afterwards he spoke and said to Ywain: Forgive
me, for I was thinking of myself. Yet not
of myself only, but of you and of many, for we
are all banished men, and we seek for the road
of our returning. And you do well on your
part, for your serving and your seeking are
one, and though you find not yet neither do
you turn aside to rest: for the time is not
come wherein you must be content with
memory and solitude.

And Ywain looked upon him and he saw
that he spoke out of sorrow: for his eyes were
like still water, but deep within them the
spirit of the man was troubled, as the sand
is troubled beneath the stillness of a spring.
And Ywain longed greatly to comfort him, but
found no words, for he would not question him
of his sorrow. Then he thought to put him

in mind of his wisdom that he had found by
loneliness: but thereto the hermit answered
yet more sadly and said: There are that choose
loneliness, but upon me it came perforce. And
for my wisdom, it is one thing to you and
another thing to me: for to you it is as a
living voice, to counsel the living, but to me
it is as the stone upon a grave, which gives
good words when there is none left to hear
them.

Then Ywain said to him: What then?
Will you return and come with me? And
the hermit smiled a little and answered him:
Not so, for I should be none the nearer to the
country of my abiding. But go you, he said,
and return to the city, and do your seeking
among men: for your life is yet to find, and
among men you must find it.

CHAPTER XXXVIII.

HOW YWAIN RETURNED AGAIN TO PALADORE FOR TO DWELL THERE, AND HOW HE SPOKE TO APPEASE A STRIFE THAT WAS BETWEEN THE PEOPLE.

So on that day Ywain had converse with the hermit, and on the morrow early he departed from him. And he went from him by the former way, but he went not after the former manner: for at this time his journeying was by daylight and not by moonlight, and he had no aid of horses but fared always upon his feet. Notwithstanding he made good speed and came betimes to the place of the stepping-stones, and it seemed to him a place right dreary and desert, where before had been his lady with him and great fight-

ing upon the bank. So he passed on quickly
and came to Paladore: and he saw the city
also as a dim and dreary city, for his heart
was fordone with loneliness and his thought
dragged like a man that is footsore with
going.

Then he came to the gate and passed in:
and immediately there came to meet him
two men, and they ran towards him on this
side and on that, and one of them was clad
in scarlet and the other in black. And they
two laid hold on him both together, and
they spoke to him loudly as it were with
one voice, so that he heard not of their
saying two words in twenty. But when
their ardour was somewhat abated, then he
heard them more plainly: and their tale was
this, that the Company of the Eagle and
the Company of the Tower were at odds
together, and some of them were even now
within the Great Hall of the city speaking
the one against the other, and like enough
to go further with it. And as for them

which took hold of Ywain, they had the office from their companies to wait within the gate, and if any should enter, to send him quickly to the place of meeting. And they offered Ywain badges, of the Tower and of the Eagle, and were urgent with him each for his own, that Ywain might declare himself as of that company: for they knew him not, or else they had forgotten, or belike they thought to carry him away with words.

And when he heard their clamouring, and knew not for what cause the striving might be, then at the first his spirit was sick within him, and he thought to break away from them. And he said to them: Let me go my way, for I have enough business of my own. And again he said: Let me go, for I am weary and would rest. But when he had spoken those words he saw the men no longer, neither the red nor the black, but he saw beside him the hermit standing and looking into his face. Then the hermit took him by the hand and began to lead

him towards the market-place: and as they
went he spoke not to Ywain, but held him
always by the hand, and it was as though
his mind was poured into Ywain's mind like
wine that is poured from one cup into another.
And Ywain knew whither he went, and he
made no more resistance, for he said within
himself: This is the life of Paladore, to
strive by companies, and I know of which
company I am. Then he thought again upon
the Eagles and his blood leapt up to be with
them, and he hastened in his going and knew
not that he hastened. And in that moment
the hermit was gone from him, and he came
alone into the market-place.

Now there was gathered in the place a
crowd exceeding great and turbulent, and
they were plainly divided between the two
companies. For they which favoured the
Tower stood upon the steps of the Great
Hall in a ground of vantage, and they which
were of the Eagles stood in the street below:
and they were waiting until their men should

come forth to them from within the Hall, and as they waited they gibbered and gibed, the one party against the other. But when they saw Ywain they left that and shouted at him all together, for they remembered him and desired him each company for their own. And the Eagles desired him because he had fought for them aforetime, and they of the Tower desired him because he had fought against them and worsted them: so that between them Ywain thought to be divided piecemeal.

But in that moment the doors of the Great Hall were opened, and they which were within began to come forth. And there came before them a crier with a bell, and he stood upon the topmost step and rang his bell and cried: and Ywain heard of his crying the last word only. And they of the Tower caught up that word and shouted joyfully: He is banished. Then the Eagles shouted: He shall not be banished; and their shouting was the louder and by some deal the fiercer. And they called to Ywain to help them, and they made way and pushed him forward upon the steps.

Then he went slowly up the steps, and he stood and looked upon the crowd: and as he stood he cast about in his mind what he should say, for of the matter in dispute he knew but this word only, that one was in danger to be banished. So from that word he began his speaking, and he said first, how that to banish any man was an evil custom, against kindness and against reason both: for if a man had done wrong he should suffer there where he had done the wrong, seeing that it was his country notwithstanding. And secondly, he said how that in any case a man should suffer by law and not by hatred: for he may offend a whole company and yet be no law-breaker, nor of evil intent. And thirdly, he said that to speak against customs is lawful: for a custom may be such as was good yesterday, but in nowise good to-day, nor for ever, and to end it is no murder.

And all this he spoke not angrily but with a sad voice and a slow: and from fierce the crowd became gentle, and they murmured continually for pleasure as a cat will purr when she is stroked with the hand. For they of Paladore love best to see fighting, but after that they love to hear speaking, and he that hath power of wind may raise their anger at his own will and lay it again, like the waters of the sea.

So they were stilled and put in peace together, as for this time, and they left the market-place and departed each to his own business. But they of the Tower forswore not their intent, for they held by their custom and hated Ywain, but they perceived well that they must abide their time.

CHAPTER XXXIX.

HOW YWAIN BEHELD A GAME OF CHILDREN AND HEARD THEIR SINGING.

Now Ywain stood still to see the crowd departing, and of them which came near to him there were some which greeted him and some which looked sullenly upon him. And as he saw them he thought upon the fashion of this world, wherein all men are homeless: for though a man dwell where he will and see good days, yet everywhere he will be at strife with some, and belike with many. Then he thought to go to his own house, and he came there and entered into it: but when he was therein he looked about him doubtfully, for he could not tell if it should be still his own, or given to another.

So he stayed not there, but went forth

again he knew not whither: for his wits
wandered otherwise, but his feet lightly
found out the ways of his desire. And the
time was the time of sunset, and there went
a great thunder over the city, and a sudden
rain; and when the rain ceased there was a
light in the air and a marvellous clearness.
And it seemed to Ywain as though that
clearness was in his eyes also, and in his
mind and in his heart: and he went wandering in joy. So he came to a gate of the
city and marked it not, but passed through
it: and beyond the gate he saw suddenly the
High Steep before him, grey and green, and
upon it was a company of children singing
and making merry, for they had run forth
after the ceasing of the rain. And there
beyond them was the sea, shining like grey
steel, and the trees were dark against it; and
the sky was heavy above with bands of purple,
but between the bands the colour of it was
pale and cool, and like to the colour of green
apples.

Then Ywain stood still to look upon the sea and the sky, and the children came round about him and looked also. And as they stood looking there passed a cloud over the Shepherdine Sands, and the cloud was drawn down upon the white water, and it was the last cloud of the storm going west before the wind. And the passing away of it was like the drawing of a curtain, for immediately there was light instead of darkness upon the Shepherdine Sands and upon all the region that was beyond. And in the light there was a land, as it were far off but exceeding clear: and upon the land was a steep and a city, and by seeming it was nc strange city, for it was built and bulwarked after the very fashion of Paladore. Notwithstanding it was strange enough: for it was small and bright as a city that is painted in a book, and the light wherewith it shone was a light of dawn and not of sunset.

And as Ywain looked upon the city it seemed to him that the light was upon his own eyes also, and upon his mind and upon his heart, and he named the land aloud and called it Aladore. And the children that were beside him heard the word that he spoke, and immediately they broke into shouting after the manner of children, and ran busily from one to another among themselves: and Ywain perceived that they would play at a game together, and by seeming the game was called the game of Aladore. And at the first he marvelled, but afterwards he marvelled no more, for he remembered how that it was forbidden to speak that name in all the city, and how that the desire of children is ever to do and to say that which is forbidden them.

Then he went a little aside and stood within the gateway and looked forth to see the playing of that pastime. And he saw how the children departed them into two bands, which stood aline the one over against the other. And their pastime was the singing of a song: and they sang it as it were an antiphony, verse answering to verse, and they kept the time full orderly with their hands and with their feet. And the verses of the song were in number six, and the words of it were these—

> To Aladore, to Aladore,
>   Who goes the pilgrim way?
> Who goes with us to Aladore
>   Before the dawn of day?
>
> O if we go the pilgrim way,
>   Tell us, tell us true,
> How do they make their pilgrimage
>   That walk the way with you?
>
> O you must make your pilgrimage
>   By noonday and by night,
> By seven years of the hard hard road
>   And an hour of starry light.
>
> O if we go by the hard hard road,
>   Tell us, tell us true,
> What shall they find in Aladore
>   That walk the way with you?
>
> You shall find dreams in Aladore,
>   All that ever were known:
> And you shall dream in Aladore
>   The dreams that were your own.

Aladore

O then, O then to Aladore,
We'll go the pilgrim way,
To Aladore, to Aladore,
Before the dawn of day.

Now these were all the verses which the children sang, but when they had sung them all, then they sang the last verse again and yet again. And as they sang they turned them about, and they went by two and by two along the edge of the green steep, after the manner of lovers or of friends which go together on pilgrimage: and when Ywain saw that his heart burned his eyes, for even in the playing of the children he beheld an image of his own life. But they went from him quickly, for they continued still in their singing and their marching, and they passed by a tower that was in the wall and Ywain saw them no more. But he heard their singing far off, when they were long gone from him, and at the last he knew not in truth whether he heard it or heard it not, but only he knew that the sound of it was still abiding with him.

CHAPTER XL.

HOW YWAIN CAME TO ALADORE.

THEN Ywain went forth again from the gateway, and he came to the edge of the High Steep, to the place wherein the children had their pastime: and there under the trees he began to go to and fro, for he was restless by reason of the song that was yet in his ears. And as he went to and fro the song continued with him, and it worked as it were an enchantment in his blood: for he kept looking upon Aladore, that lay there under the sky border, beyond the Shepherdine Sands, and he saw it in a light that was no light of earth. And he knew no longer where he might be, but the world was lost and vanisht from him; and his feet ceased from going, and he stood at gaze, looking only upon that land of his desire.

Now at the first it was far off from him, but afterwards he beheld it near and clear past telling, for it seemed to him that power came upon him whereby he had vision of things not to be seen with eyes. And for the land, he saw that it was in all ways like to the land whereon he stood, and in like shape it lay beside the sea margent, and in like manner it rose up in a high steep, green and grey, and set with tall trees and shadowy. And for the city, that also was of no strange semblance, for it was in fashion the very image and counterpart of Paladore: and it was compassed with like walls and towers, and with like gardens and streets enriched and diapered.

But by imagination Ywain beheld the place otherwise; for in his vision he perceived it as a city of peace, and one that knew neither strife nor evil custom, nor men of wood nor men of wildfire, but only young lovers and old friends and folk of free and gentle dealing. And besides these there were none other, save only fays and phantoms: and Ywain knew that it was in all things such a city as seeing it he would have loved it in his youth, and his life-days seemed to him but wasted until he should enter and dwell therein. And therewith his spirit rose within him and cried after that land with utter longing, for his memory and his hope were become one, and he knew not how to endure them.

Then he started suddenly out of his vision and went down the High Steep like a rolling stone, and he came quickly with great bounds to the margent of the sea. And when he came there he was aware of a little ship that lay upon the water, and it was made fast to the shore with a black rope and a white, and in it was a mast and a sail, and the sail was party black and white. And Ywain stayed not there, but leapt aboard and hoised up the sail: and he took the hermit's knife from his breast and cut through the ropes, both the black and the white, for they were knotted strongly upon a ring of iron. Then he took the tiller into his hand, and the ship began to go swiftly from the shore. And he looked towards Aladore, and saw it fair before him: but how he should come there he knew not, for he must come first into that white and tumbling water of the Shepherdine Sands.

Right so he came flying amidst the Sands and entered into the quick of them: and the ship staggered and went suddenly from under him, and he fell down and down to the bottom of the sea. And he fell flatling, and sprang up again and leapt upon his feet: and he looked upward, and beheld the sea, as it were above his head, all white and seething. And he perceived how it was in truth no sea but mist, and belike it was a mist of faery, for it rolled and swirled above him in all semblance like to the sea, but there was in it neither death nor darkness.

Then he went forward under the mist, and as he went it broke and was made thin before him, and he saw green grass beneath his feet, and over against him a mount of grey and green, and he knew that he was come unto the High Steep of Aladore. And he saw it with no amazement but with gladness only, for it was with him as with a man that has been long voyaging and is returning at last into his own country. And he loved the land and greeted it in his heart; and he found the path and climbed upon it, and came quickly to the topmost of the Steep.

And as he went climbing, he heard again the song that before was in his ears, and at the first he knew not whether he heard it within him or without. Then he saw above him the walls of the city and the gate therein, and before the gate were children playing, and the children were the same children and their pastime was the same pastime: for they stood aline in two lines and sang together after the former fashion, and the words of their song were these—

> You shall find dreams in Aladore,
>   All that ever were known:
> And you shall dream in Aladore
>   The dreams that were your own.

Then when he heard those words he assented thereto, and he laughed in his heart and so passed on: for they seemed to him nothing new, but he heard them as it were out of childhood and sweet memory. And he entered by the gateway and came singing into the city; and the streets of it were cool and shining like pale gold, for they were all agleam with a light mist of sunrise.

CHAPTER XLI.

HOW YWAIN ENTERED INTO THE RHYMER'S
HERITAGE, AND HOW HE FOUND HIS LADY
THEREIN.

Now as Ywain went into the city he went
joyfully, for his heart was uplifted, and his
thoughts were like high white clouds in a
blue sky of summer. And most of all he
joyed to see the beauty of the place, for the
form of it was the form of Paladore, but the
beauty was mingled of likeness and unlike-
ness. And wherever he looked, there he saw
that which he remembered, and there also
he saw that which he remembered not, so
that his joy was both old and new.

And when he had gone but a score of
paces into the city, he came to the court
that lay before the great Gard, and in the
entrance of it he stayed. And there passed

258

by him two or three which went not in:
and he asked them whose was the castle,
for he perceived that there was a change
upon it. And they answered him that it
was no castle, but the Rhymer's Hall; for
that by the Rhymer it was long since founded
and upbuilt. And when they had so answered they vanished from him suddenly, and
were gone as though they had never been.

Then he was astonished and pondered a
little, looking within the court. And in the
court he saw not the halberdiers and men
a-horseback which had been there aforetime,
but upon the steps of the castle he saw a
five or six minstrels with their lutes, and
anon they sang and anon they talked together, and by seeming their talk was all
only upon their lutes and upon their singing.

Then Ywain came to them and greeted
them, and said: How long is this become a
place of singing? And one of them answered
him courteously, and said: Fair lord, by your
will we sing and by your will we are silent,
seeing that we are but the servants of your

dream. And even as Ywain heard those
words the minstrels vanished, and there was
nothing of them left in that place, save a
little sound of lutestrings that lingered waywardly.

So Ywain entered into the Rhymer's Hall,
and within door he found the porter, and the
man sat there reading upon a book. And
Ywain asked him: What read you? and immediately the porter vanished without answer
given, and there was nought seen of him but
his chair, and upon the chair was the book
whereon he had been reading. Then Ywain
came near and took up the book and looked
within it: and it was a wide book, painted
delicately with great letters and with pictures.
And the picture that was open before him
was the picture of two lovers by a garden
door; and the lady stood beside the door
and leaned upon it with her hand to open
it, but the lover came to her in habit of a
pilgrim, and his hat was broad above his
face, and shadowed it. And Ywain's heart
quickened as he looked: for the lady was his

own lady, and she stood there as living as the leaves in spring.

Then he laid the book upon the chair and left it lying, and he went through the Rhymer's Hall from end to end, and through all the courts of it and out beyond. And he came by a pleached alley to a close, and looked across the close: and upon the far side of it was a wall of stone, and in the wall was a carven doorway, and a door of wood. And there before the doorway stood Aithne in the morning gold, and she laid her hand against the door and looked a little downward, as one that is waiting and musing. And when Ywain came to her she spoke no word, but she turned away and led him through the doorway, and the door fell back and closed behind them: and it closed full slowly, but at the last there was a small noise of clanking and the bar went home into the notch.

And that noise was sweet in Ywain's ears, for it seemed to shut the world away, and he went to his lady as one that comes to

his own land after long captivity. And little
they spoke in words, but they looked each
at other, and his eyes were to her like two
bright spears levelled in battle, and her eyes
were to him like a valley at evening, when
the smoke goes up into the twilight.

Then at the last he said to her: What
then is this place? And she said: It was
the Rhymer's heritage, and now is mine; and
that which is mine is yours, for you have
found it out and taken it. And belike it
was yours from the beginning, for it is you
that have made it anew, and you are the
master of your dream. And as she spoke
those words a fear came suddenly upon him
lest she also should vanish and be gone from
him. And he would have cried aloud of his
fear, but she laid her hand upon his mouth
and laughed and stayed him from uttering.
And she said: I know your thought, and
vain it is: for your dream and mine are one
and not two, as they were aforetime, but each
in other we have our home and our abiding.

CHAPTER XLII.

HOW YWAIN AND AITHNE WERE GIVEN EACH TO OTHER, AND HOW THEY WERE WEDDED BY THE FREEDOM OF ALADORE.

THEN Ywain stood still and mused, looking down upon the grass about his feet: and he mused upon his pilgrimage whereby he had at last come hither. And Aithne asked him of his musing, and he answered her not, but he said: Tell me, O my beloved, when shall be the end of this my pilgrimage? And she answered: It is ended, for the shrine is found, and the lamp of the world is lit afresh. But he asked her again: By what token shall I have certainty of this? And she said: By a flame and by a gift, for by those tokens is love confirmed of all lovers both of old and for ever. Then his blood beat and his throat trembled and he said: Yea, beloved, but it may yet be far to the hour of giving. And she also trembled and said: The hour of giving is the hour of starlight, and between the sunsetting and the moonrising it will be here. Then Ywain looked again upon the ground and he saw beside his feet the long morning shadows, and he said: It is far, O my beloved. And she said: Nay, but have I not told you, that all things here are yours, for that you only are the master of the dream?

Then with her hand she pointed to the shadows upon the grass, and they were two shadows that were as one, and they lay upon a wide and open space. And Ywain looked again upon them and was amazed: for the shadows drew in apace, and they went round him as the finger goes upon the dial, save that they went a forty times more quickly. And he asked of his lady: What mean these shadows, for they are gone from the West into the East. And she answered him softly:

O my lord, see you not that you are master
even of the sun in heaven? And she looked
stilly into his eyes, and a little wind of evening blew cool upon him.

Then she took him by the hand and led
him within the house, and she brought him
to an upper room and to a window therein
which looked upon the city. And the window
was wide open, and without it was a gallery
of stone; and Ywain held his lady's hand
and went forward upon the gallery. Then
he looked down, and saw beneath him the
courtyard full of folk, and the place was filled
with the thronging of them, and the street
beyond the gates was filled also. And at the
first the folk were silent and shadowy, and
the twilight gathered thick upon them: and
Ywain looked hard among them, peering to
see if by their faces he might know them.
And by one and by two he knew them, and
there were by seeming in that place the faces
of all men and women that he had known
in all his life-days.

Then pity came upon him in a moment, and great pain: for he saw them as folk lost and gone from him, and he would have had them to be partakers in his joy. And in that moment came a light of sunset into the sky, and it glowed upon the faces of them that were before him: and they cried all together and called him by his name, giving him friendship and honour. And Ywain shut to his eyes, for there was that which burned them hotly: and when he looked forth again there was neither face nor form of any man, but only a sound as of folk departing.

Then Ywain said to Aithne: Are there not also some within doors in this place, that I may do them courtesy? And she answered: They, too, are of the bordure of your dream. So she brought him within, and they went towards the great hall, and there went with them lights and trumpets. And when they came to the hall they found there a great company of knights sitting at feast together: and the knights were in number a hundred, and they were all they which in their time had sought the Lady Aithne and her love, and their feasting was full sombre and courteous. And when they saw Ywain and Aithne they rose up and did them reverence, and they gathered about them and spoke many things of honour and of farewell.

Then Ywain gave them thanks with the like honour, and immediately they faded from before him, and with them the lights also faded and fell to darkness. And in the hall was none left with Ywain and Aithne, save one child only: and the child was nowise strange to them, for it was he which had been the beginner of their pilgrimage. And in his hand was a torch burning, and he bore it up before them, and about them the shadows went dancing upon the walls and upon the roof: and he went down the hall, and they two followed after him with hand in hand, and so he brought them to the chamber where they should be wed. And when they were come there he turned his torch downwards to quench it upon the floor: and the flame of it vanished and the child therewith, and the place was lit by starlight only.

But in the chamber was also a little glowing as of embers, and Ywain saw there an altar of bronze: and it seemed to him right ancient, as a thing made in the time out of mind. And beside the altar was a platter of meal and a cup of red wine standing: and Aithne took the meal into her hand, and in like manner Ywain took the wine. And they two stood beside the altar on this side and on that, and sprinkled it with meal and wine; and there went up from it two bright flames of fire, a red and a white, and they spired up and were entwined together so that they were two colours but one only flame.

Then Ywain looked upon his beloved and said: The flame is here truly, but where is the gift? And she also looked steadfastly upon him and answered him: The gift is here, but it is yours to show first the manner of the giving. And thereat he took her by the hand and said: Here in free marriage I give thee the body of me, my life with thy life, my blood with thy blood, my dust with thy dust to be mingled and made one. Then with a low voice she said after him the same words. And he said again: Here also I give thee the heart of me, my love with thy love, my hope with thy hope, my sorrow with thy sorrow to be mingled and made one. And those words also she spoke in like manner. Then he said the third time: Here also do I witness that I have given thee long since the spirit of me, to be thy friend and fellow to the end of pilgrimage. Yea, she said, and thereafter: and with thee and with all spirits to be mingled and made one.

Then she said again as to herself only: Now am I wedded by the freedom of Aladore, and so is my promise fulfilled. And when she had said that she fell suddenly to weeping. And she went to the window and leaned upon the sill, and Ywain came near, and he saw her tears falling bright under the starlight.

269

Aladore

And he was both sorry and afraid, and he took her in his arms and asked her many times wherefore she wept, and she told him not. And at the last she said: That will I tell you, but not now: and I weep not for sorrow but for remembrance. Then he solaced her with comfort of strength and of silence: and afterwards they went joyfully to their wedding and to their rest. And the moon rose on Aladore, and they saw her not: for they slept as it had been the sleep of childhood.

CHAPTER XLIII.

HOW AITHNE SHOWED YWAIN OF THE ENCHANTMENTS OF THE RHYMER, AND OF THEM WHICH DO THEREAFTER.

So in this wise Ywain and Aithne fulfilled their youth, and they entered into newness of life. And they endured no more the fear of time, for in Aladore are days and seasons, but no count of them: and there is there neither change nor perishing.

Now on a day it befell that they two stood together at dawn, looking upon the sea: and the sun rose out of the sea and went swiftly up the sky. And Ywain looked upon the sea, and he saw it bright and clear even to the farthest border, and there was neither land nor cloud upon it, but gold only and a void space above the gold. And thereat he was astonished, and he asked of Aithne: Where then is Paladore? for I came thence by no long voyage. And she smiled a little and answered him: Let be, dear love, for it is not far off: and as much thereof as was yours, so much is yours still, for so much you brought hither when you came. And this is the law of Aladore, that in it hath every man his own and nothing less: yea rather he hath more, for unto his own vision are added many great enchantments. Then said Ywain: Which be these enchantments? And she answered: They are the enchantments of the Rhymer, that was a wizard indeed: and his magic he left to all such as are able for it, unto the world's end; and many there be of them.

Then she took Ywain up into a high tower, and so forth upon the battlements thereof, and she said: Look now and behold the sorrows of Gudrun, for she loved much and suffered many things, and her end was full of right piteous remembrance. And Ywain looked down from the battlements, and he saw a steep coast and a river which ran swiftly to a western sea. And there lay hard by the river a steading upon a knole amidst the vale, and it nourished plenteously both sheep and kine. And an old man he saw which dwelt therein, and five boys that were his sons, and one more that was his brother's son : and all they went among the cattle, and rode by hill and by dale. And Ywain looked further, by a seven mile, and he saw yet another steading amidst the grey slopes, and there also was an old man dwelling, and five sons, and a daughter thereto : and these men likewise went among the cattle and rode by hill and by dale, and the maiden tended them within the hall. And Ywain saw how the folk would come and go between the steadings, and how in their dealing there would be love and strife among them.

Then Aithne asked of him : What see you ?

And he told her of that which he saw. And she said: Not so shall be your vision, for though by your deeming these are but country folk, and their land a little land and a barren, yet is your deeming vain, and their life is greater than you know. Look therefore again, and by enchantment shall your eyes be made clear to see them.

Then Ywain looked again, and as he looked a voice was in his ears, and his heartstrings rung deeply thereto, for they were plucked and quivering as beneath the hand of a strong harper. And now he saw that land after another fashion: for he saw it as a strange and awful land, and the folk of it as a folk beset with fearful things, yet fearing nought, as men in the hollow of God's hand. And as folk loving and beloved he saw them, and strong and uncomplaining and compassionate, yet also working wild deeds, after the manner of men. For he saw young Kiartan the Icelander, and Bodli that was his friend and fellow, and Gudrun that was beloved of them both: and the double skein of their love was tangled and broken in his sight.

And first the voice showed him all the love of Kiartan and Gudrun, and how Kiartan came daily from Herdholt by moor and dale unto the house of Bathstead, wherein Gudrun dwelt: and how her heart fluttered joyfully at hearing of his footfall: and long they talked together, and at evening departed hardly each from other. And their very parting was sweet, for in that moment the veil of time would fall away from before them, so that they saw love whole and without cloud.

Then the voice bade Ywain see the pride of Kiartan, whereby he went adventuring over sea. And he saw how Kiartan came across the foam to Norroway, and there lingered by the space of three good years, making pastime of another love. And that was the love of Ingibiorg, that was King Olaf's daughter: yet at the last he left her also and returned, howbeit he returned not till it was too late.

And the voice showed Ywain all the sorrows of Bodli, Thorleik's son: for he was of all her lovers the man which most loved Gudrun. And Ywain saw him come alone from Norroway with tidings of Kiartan and of Ingibiorg: and thereby he wedded Gudrun and fulfilled his longing and his doom.

Then Ywain's heart trembled with pity and with terror: for he saw how Kiartan came again after three years, and found Gudrun gone from him utterly and given to his friend. And upon Kiartan also came despair, as it had come before upon Gudrun: so that he turned him to Refna and wedded where he had no heart's desire. And thereafter fell great bitterness between Herdholt and Bathstead, and though there was love still between Bodli and Kiartan, yet was there death also by the custom of men.

For on a dark road among the hills came Kiartan riding with two more: and there met him all the five brothers of Gudrun, and Bodli with them. And Ywain saw how Kiartan fought strongly with Gudrun's kin, and Bodli stood apart: yet at the last he might not forsake the men of his own house. And he drew near the fighting and thrust his sword into the side of Kiartan whom he loved. And Ywain knew that he had slain therewith his own soul also.

Then said the voice to Ywain that he should look once more upon Gudrun, for that she lived long afterwards when the rest were gone their way. And Ywain saw her as an old and sightless dame, and she sat within her bower at evening. And it was summer, with hay in field, and the carles sang as they went homeward: and the sea murmured below, and above was a chapel on the hill, with bells which rang therein. And Gudrun sat there with her son, that was the son of Bodli: and he asked her of those whom she had loved, which was most loved. And she told him in no plain words, but in a dark

and sorrowful saying: for she that was blind
and old saw again Herdholt and her youth,
and the deeds that she had done therein.

Then the voice ceased, and the vision:
and Ywain looked upon Aithne. And he
would have spoken, but he could not, for his
voice was choked within his throat. And
she smiled tenderly upon him, as one that
has understanding of pain, and therewith she
gave her hand into his hand: and presently
he spoke and said: What is this place, and
whose is the voice which I heard?

And she said: It is the Rhymer's Tower,
and the voice is the voice of one which had
the Rhymer's magic. For there are here
many voices, and all to your solace: and by
them is the world re-made after the fashion
of life enduring.

CHAPTER XLIV.

HOW YWAIN BEHELD HIS LADY SLEEPING, AND HOW HE DESIRED TO SEE THE CASTLE OF KERIOC.

So Ywain dwelt in a land of enchantments, and had his will thereof continually. And many things he devised for his joyance, and one thing beyond all other. For it befell him on a day that he awoke at dawn, and thereafter came the sunrise and made light the chamber where he was. And he turned him and looked upon Aithne, thereas she lay still sleeping: and her face was fresh and clear and tranquil as the face of a little maid in her flower of youth. And as Ywain looked upon her his heart was pricked through with a sudden pain: for he saw her as she had

279

been aforetime, in the days when she was
no lady of his. And the pain was sharp,
for wellnigh he forgot that which he knew
of her, and thought only on that which he
knew not, and he perceived that he could
never come thereto, except he should go
behind the back of time.

Then Aithne awoke and saw him looking
down upon her, and she said: O my beloved,
why look you so darkly upon me? And he
said: Great things have you given me, and
great enchantments have you showed me,
but one thing I lack that you have held
from me. Then she asked of him: What
have I held from you, or what will you ask
of me that I will not give you presently?
And he was glad of that word and made
request of her, saying: I beseech you that
you bring me into the Castle of Kerioc,
wherein you were born and nurtured: for
except I see the manner of your youth
therein I am not wholly mingled with your
life.

Aladore

And when she heard him she laughed and loved him in her heart, for that which he asked was pleasing to her. And she said to him: Go now and have your will, for your request is granted you. And you shall go by the way of yesterday, and enter into the garden close and come thence into the place beyond. And you shall stand therein, looking upon the ground and speaking no word save one word that is your name, and that you shall say aloud by a hundred times and one. So prove your adventure and come again to me; for until you come I am alone.

Then Ywain kissed her thrice and went out: and he went by the way of the garden close and came to the place beyond. And he stood and looked downward upon the ground and spoke his own name aloud, and when he had spoken it but a score of times then his name was his name no longer, but a sound without sense and void. And he knew that the place was changed wherein he stood: and he looked up and saw the sea hard by him, and by the sea was a castle both great and ancient. And he went forward boldly and entered into the castle without help or hindrance.

Then he went spying out all things within the castle, and he found it rich and well beseen: and folk there were therein, but they took no heed of him, no more than if he had not been. And at the last he heard a voice singing and coming towards him: and presently there came to him a little maid. And she left singing, and looked curiously upon him, as one that knew him not. Then his heart was buffeted within him, for she was the maid which he sought, but he perceived that she had of him neither love nor knowledge.

And he said to her: Of a surety you are Aithne: but where is she which is my lady in Aladore? And the child looked upon him with clear eyes, and she answered him in a little voice and sweet: Sir Stranger, you come

hither too late: for long ago she is grown up
and gone away.

Then fear came upon him, and he longed to
be with his own again: and he woke as from a
vain dream, and stood in his chamber whence
he had gone forth. And before him was his
lady in her own image, and her kisses were
still upon his lips: and she lay looking upon
him in the sunlight and her eyes were filled
with love and with laughter.

CHAPTER XLV.

HOW YWAIN FOUND AGAIN HIM WHICH WAS FORGOTTEN IN ALADORE, AND HOW HE HEARD A RING OF BELLS AT MIDNIGHT.

THEREAFTER came Ywain many times into the castle of Kerioc, and Aithne with him. For she loved greatly to have him there, notwithstanding that she had good game at him when he went thither the first time: and in especial she would have him there in winter at the time of Yule. For that castle stands by the very margent of the sea upon a high rock; and it is in fashion like to an island, for on the one side it is set high above the land and on the other side it goes down steeply toward the shore. And the wind of winter goes over it from the land seaward: and on the shore is warm lying among the sand-hills which are beneath the castle. And above the sand-hills is a postern gate and steps of stone: and thereby came Ywain and Aithne many times unto the shore at midnight, that they might see the stars and hear the crying of the birds. For the sea-birds cry about that place with a sweet cry and a sad, and in the darkness they draw near and are not seen, as it were the souls of the beloved.

So after this wise Ywain and Aithne came and went, and they took of all seasons such days as they would, and lived carelessly: for they were as those which have more than they can spend. And after certain times it was so with Ywain that he remembered no longer the days when he knew not Kerioc; for his life was changed and deepened as a river is deepened when twain flow together in one. And he desired no more, save that he might always so continue: for he forgot that the road of his pilgrimage was not yet passed beyond the gateway of death, yet at the last he remembered it perforce.

For upon a day he wandered alone in the

castle of Kerioc, and by chance he came into a crypt that was thereunder; and in the crypt he spied a door, which was well locked and made fast so that he could not open it. Then he came to Aithne and said: What is this door, whereof you gave me not the key? For all other keys she had given him save this one only. And she denied not, but answered him plainly, and she counselled him that he should forbear that door. But when she saw that he would not forbear then she gave him the key, and she said to him: Go now and take your way, for it is a man's way, and it may be that your heart shall be stronger than your head to serve you. And if not, then must I endure it, for I knew long since how this should be. And Ywain perceived how she spoke to him; and she spoke with love and mirth, and in the mirth was a little sorrow: but he put by the sorrow and took hold on the mirth, and so kissed her and went his way. And he came to the door and opened it, and within were bare chambers of rock, in manner of dungeons. And in one chamber he perceived a dim light, and when he was come there he saw a lamp of bronze hanging, and beneath it an old man on a chair of black stone; and his beard was long and white, and it fell over his knees as a stream falls over a mountain-side. And when he saw him Ywain trembled, for his heart misgave him who the old man should be.

Then Ywain said to him: Sir, forgive me, for I came hither unknowing. And the old man answered him: My son, this long time that you have been in Aladore, you do all things unknowing. And Ywain said thereto: Yet my life I know, and my own gladness: for this a man cannot but know, and it suffices me. Then the old man looked hard upon Ywain, and his eyes were like grey stones, and the weight of them sank into Ywain's eyes and lay heavy upon his heart. And he said to Ywain: You speak also unknowing, for in Aladore is no substance of truth, but all is dream. And this for you is Kerioc, and the seventh winter that you are herein: but I tell you that all is dream. For since you forgot Paladore it is not yet seven days : and as for Kerioc it is there where it was aforetime, beside the forest of Broceliande.

Then Ywain hardened his heart, and he said to the old man : Sir, I have heard your saying and I understand it not : for I am here, and in my right mind, and therein is the substance of truth for every man. And the old man said : Not so, but you shall awake and know your dream. And I will give you a token : and the token shall be when you shall hear the bells of Paladore ringing midnight in your ears.

Then was Ywain angered against the old man, for he feared his saying : and he left him suddenly and went out, and locked the door fiercely upon him. And he came to Aithne and said no word : and she perceived how he was lost in trouble. Then she spoke gently to him : Tell me your thought, for I perceive that you have found again him that was forgotten. Then Ywain told her of the old man and of his great beard, and of his eyes, and of his evil saying : and he told her with many words, for he was angry and afraid. And she also was afraid, for she had seen that old man aforetime, and found no force against him. But now she took her lute and made a song of him: and when he heard the song then was Ywain brought again into his former mind, as for that time, but Aithne doubted within herself.

Then within a while the day drew in and the sun set on Kerioc and on all the lands of Aladore. And Ywain and Aithne laid them to their rest: and Aithne slept deep and stirred not, but Ywain awoke suddenly. And he found darkness on all things and no light at all, for moon there was none, and the stars were hid in mist. And for a while he lay still and moved not, but his mind moved continually, and it led him hither and thither until he was perplexed and weary. And in an evil moment he thought on that old man which he had seen: and instantly he heard a sound of bells, and he knew that they were the bells of Paladore, for they were sounding midnight. Then he started up in fear and went softly out of the chamber, for he said within himself that he would walk upon the shore and come again, and so ease him of his thought.

So he came to the postern and opened it, and went down upon the sand-hills, and he wandered to and fro thereon without respect of mind or body: and at the last he was fordone with weariness, and set him down to rest, and right so he fell to forgetfulness and sleep. And when he awoke the second time it was grey dawn, and the mist was still upon the sea: and he turned him about and looked up that he might see the castle of Kerioc. And he saw neither shape nor sign of it, nor any way of his returning: but he saw instead a high steep, grey and green, and walls and towers thereon. Then the mist began to depart from before his eyes, and he knew the place as a man knows again the face which he had forgotten. And his heart failed within him, and the sun rose on Paladore.

CHAPTER XLVI.

HOW YWAIN WAS COUNSELLED OF THE PRINCE OF PALADORE.

THEN Ywain came to the height of the steep, and there before the gate he stood in doubt, for he knew not whither he should go. And in his doubt his feet drew him unwittingly, and he looked up suddenly and saw the Great Gard and the courtyard which was before it. And the courtyard was as it had been afore-time, with halberdiers before the door and men a-horseback in their armour: and the Rhymer's Hall and the minstrels and all his dealings therein seemed but an old vision or a show which had passed into memory. Not-withstanding he doubted even of his misery: for he said within himself: Surely this also is a dream, and there beyond the garden close is my lady waiting until I come to her.

Then he went towards the door, and one came thereout to meet him: and Ywain perceived that it was Sir Rainald, and he would have passed by with such courtesy as might suffice. But Sir Rainald stayed him and took him by the hand, and he said to Ywain how that it was even he whom he sought and none other: for the Prince would speak with him of certain matters. And of these matters, he said, I will tell you this much, by way of friendship: and namely, that the Prince, which is your master and liege, takes it ill that he is so deceived in you. For you gave him assurance that you would dwell in Paladore, and do after the customs of the city: but now you deal otherwise and are gone continually from hence, and none knows whither.

Then Ywain was perplexed and knew not what he should answer: for he remembered how that it was forbidden in that city to speak the name of Aladore. Also he remembered the saying of the hermit, that he must return to Paladore and find his life among men and so come to the land of his desire. And Sir Rainald kept watch upon him slyly out of the side of his eye, and he saw his perplexity and in part he knew the reason of it. And he said to Ywain: Go now, and follow the counsel of a friend; and say what you will unto the Prince, save only that you say not any thing which is outrageous against our custom. For even to utter such a word before a Prince is ungentle, seeing that he is not bred to hear villainy and hath no skill to answer thereto.

So Ywain went from him and came presently before the Prince; and the Prince was counting his money: for he was a careful man, and every month he counted his money from one great chest into another. And at the first he looked upon Ywain and gave him no greeting, but afterwards when he had made an end of his counting then he spoke to him. And he said as Sir Rainald had reported him, how that he was deceived in Ywain: for he had looked to have him dwelling continually in Paladore, to fight and to do adventures, and not to go wandering otherwhere.

Then Ywain answered him courteously and said: Sir, I have done with my wandering, and except it be in Paladore I have no place of dwelling, as in this world. And when he had said that the Prince looked shrewdly upon him, as one that would pierce a covered thing, and he asked of Ywain: Whither then go you, and whence came you now? For you have been seven days in hiding, since that you were seen within the city. And Ywain answered: Sir, it is hard to tell: for I have been in no place of the world, but in a land of dreams. Ha! said the Prince, I knew it well, for it is a common case and an evil. And I will deal patiently with you in this matter, seeing that you are an outlander born and not yet perfect in the custom of our city. Know then that in Paladore a dream is a thing of nought and a byword of folly, for we are lovers of truth, and in dreams is no truth at all. And we approve all such things as have substance, and gold the chief and sign of all: and thereby is the repute of them which are great among us. For to do and to have is the virtue of men, but they which dream do nothing and gain no pennyworth.

And Ywain could well hear that which was said, for it was clearly spoken: but in the same moment he heard also his lady's voice and remembered him of her sweet fellowship. And his heart grew hot and his eyes were lightened: and the Prince faded suddenly from before him and the gold was turned to sunshine within the chest. And Ywain turned him about toward the doorway, and he saw there Aithne in the beauty of morning: and she smiled and said to him: Beloved, why went you from me: for I dreamed evilly of bells at midnight, and I awoke and found you not.

CHAPTER XLVII.

HOW YWAIN AND AITHNE HAD SIGHT OF HUBERT, AND RETURNED TOGETHER INTO PALADORE.

Now was Ywain again in Aladore and accompanied with his love: and for a while he forgot the Prince and all his counsel, and went among divers delights as a honey-bee goes among a wilderness of flowers. And it befell on a night that he sat with Aithne beside a fountain, and in the pool of the fountain they looked upon the summer stars. And round about them were cypresses and shadows, and there was no wind in the hollow of the night nor any sound save a little silvery sound of the fountain.

And Aithne spoke softly to Ywain in the dark, and she said to him: Beloved, tell me of many things, for the night is still and secret, and this fountain shall be your fountain of memory. And he asked her for asking's sake: Of which thing first shall I tell you? and she answered: Of your life in Paladore, and of those with whom you had your dealing, whether in love or in hate, for some of them I also have known and some never: and they shall be to me like them which are in a tale of faery, or a picture woven upon the wall.

Then Ywain leaned over and looked into the pool of the fountain, and he remembered the saying of the hermit, how that in all still water there will be visions. And true it was aforetime and true now: and in this water Ywain saw both Paladore and all that he had done therein. And the faces of his friends he saw, and of his enemies, and he saw his own face and form among them, and he perceived all their love and their evil malice. And that which he saw he told it to Aithne as a tale out of live memory, for it was there before his eyes in clear colours. And he told her of those four which had been friends to him in Paladore: and namely of Maurice which had a merry wit, and of Dennis whose sayings bit like salt. Also of Bartholomy the religious and of Hubert that first of all named Aladore to Ywain by name: and Ywain made a more especial mention of Hubert, because that he was such an one as would give the world for a dream. And ever as he rehearsed of Hubert, Ywain saw his face more clear before him: and when he had come to an end of his tale then he saw him yet more clear. And Ywain fell silent and bent him down above the water, for he remembered the well of the hermit, and he thought to see not only that which had befallen, but also somewhat of that which should befall. But Aithne knew his thought and said to him: Look no more, for this is the fountain of memory, and though the memory be not ours but greater, yet in it are shown no deeds save those which are accomplished.

Notwithstanding Ywain continued looking, and as he looked he cried out in anger, for he saw in the vision Sir Rainald, and how he came with certain of his and laid hold on Hubert: and they led Hubert away by force and so passed as it were out of the pool into the dimness of the night. Then Ywain started up, and told Aithne of that which he had seen: and she said: You do well to cry out, howbeit you cry too late, for that which you saw is surely done already. But Ywain stood staring into the darkness, for it seemed to him that he heard a going among the cypresses.

And as he stood there staring, and Aithne with him, there came one walking toward them in the thickest of the shadows: and when he was come nearer he lift up his face and looked steadfastly at them, and so passed by and was gone from them again. And Aithne said to Ywain: Tell me quickly, whose face was that which I saw. And Ywain drew in his breath and answered her:

It was the face of Hubert, and though he
spoke no word, yet with his eyes he called
me. Yea, said Aithne, and methought he
called us both : for he looked upon me also,
and in his look was strong sorrow and entreaty. Then pity and anger went over Ywain
like a river in flood, and he said to his lady :
What must I do, for I have need of your
help and your enchantments.

Then Aithne answered him not, but she
took him by the hand and brought him to
the margent of the fountain. And they held
firmly each by other, and so stepped together
into the pool : and Ywain felt the water cold
about his knees. And he shivered and awoke
as it were from a sleep : and the fountain
and the cypresses were vanished from him
and he stood with Aithne upon a beach of
the sea. And before them was a high steep,
shining with grey and with green : and above
it was a grey and silver cloud, and a cres-
cent moon, and the moon rose over Paladore.

CHAPTER XLVIII.

HOW YWAIN WAS AWEARIED OF PALADORE, AND HOW HE WAS MISHANDLED BY THE GREAT ONES OF THE CITY.

THEN they climbed the Steep together and entered into the city: and Ywain brought Aithne home to his own house. And he made her a little supper, scant enough, and drew wine for her of the wine which the Eagles had given him: and sweet it was still, but the spirit was gone out of it. And when they had eaten and drunk, then a great weariness came upon Ywain, and he spoke, and uttered his complaint unto Aithne: for he was adread to hear ill tidings of Hubert, and in his heart he sighed after the peace of Aladore. And his lady comforted him and

301

said: Beloved, think not to be alone in weariness, for to me also the business of Paladore hath been as dust upon the tongue. But this is the fortune of men, to dwell in two realms, until that our life is changed: and it may be that the time is not long. And what matter, if by our own magic we may come and go? and what grief, if we may be together?

So Ywain was comforted by means of those words, for they were more than wine to him: and the chime told midnight, and they twain laid them to their sleep. And in the morning before men were stirring Ywain ran quickly to the house of Hubert and knocked upon the door: and there came to him Maurice and Dennis, and told him ill tidings of Hubert, how that he had been thrust forth out of the city, never to return under pain of life. And they told him further how that the Eagles were sworn to bring him in again: for he had done no wrong, but only to speak against them of the Tower. And Ywain had great indignation thereat, and swore instantly to be of their fellowship; but inwardly he groaned to be so bound again, for he saw no end to strife and no day of returning.

Notwithstanding he stooped him to his burden and shouldered it: and he went here and there throughout the city and spoke among divers sorts of men. And in general he found them to be of three sorts: and namely, there were some of good will toward the Eagles, and some which held by the Tower, for favour's sake: and yet more there were which were men of ease and loved nothing so much as to keep order and custom and to hear no questions. And these said to Ywain that they were neither of this side nor of that, but would favour no man that should be a disturber of peace.

Then came one to Ywain and stayed him in the midst of the street: and he was a Summoner, and by his office he summoned Ywain to come before the Archbishop. So Ywain went with him, and as he went he marvelled within himself what manner of turn was this, for he had had no dealings with clergy, neither for them neither against.

And when he came to the palace then he was yet more astonished : for the Archbishop sat in no public place but in a little chamber set about with books, and with him were three or four great ones of the company of the Tower. And they greeted Ywain courteously and asked him to speak his mind unto them concerning Hubert. Then Ywain took the word and reasoned with them, that it was no good cause to banish a man, if he should have spoken against a company or against a custom. And when he had said that, he looked to be down-cried and angrily used.

Howbeit the game was otherwise played, as at this time, for none cried out nor used him angrily, but they of the Tower made a show to receive his saying courteously and to agree thereto. Then the Archbishop spoke to Ywain, and his eyes glowed like coals, and his voice was rich and sweet like strong wine softened with honey, and he said : These are my friends and yours, and they would be friends to Hubert also, for there is no malice in them, but good will and free forgiveness. But Hubert would not, to my grief I say it: for he was taken with an ill mind and brought disease upon many. And his disease was this, that he became a dreamer of dreams, and would have others to be like himself: and thereby they were in danger to have perished.

Then said Ywain: My lord, I pray you pardon me: of what dreams do men perish? And the Archbishop answered him patiently and said: Surely of all such dreams as are not according to faith. Then said Ywain: I rejoice to hear my lord's saying, for Hubert is of all men most full of faith, as one that would give the world for a dream. And even as he does, so do I and mine: for we long after our own land, and go pilgrimage to find it. And in that it is a land of dream it is a land of faith: for by our dreams we make life new and ever during, and what else do all the men of faith?

And when he said that the Archbishop was some deal choked in his throat, and the red blood came into his face about his eyes. And he said to Ywain: What mean you, sir, for I fear lest I should understand your saying. And Ywain answered: Let me use plain words with reverence: for we are both of us men and the sons of men, and to each man his own magic. And we all seek for the land of our desire, and we build therein a city and a house for our abiding. And you call your city Paradise, and ours we call Aladore, for of our own dreams it is builded and upheld.

Then the Archbishop rose up upon his feet, and he looked on Ywain with a stern countenance, and said: It is enough. And he went out in his wrath, and the great ones followed after him.

CHAPTER XLIX.

HOW YWAIN WAS EXCOMMUNICATE AFTER THE CUSTOM OF PALADORE.

LITTLE enough thought Ywain of the anger of those great ones, for he held himself to have outreasoned them, and he perceived not how by his cunning the Archbishop had entrapped him before witnesses of repute. But Aithne perceived it, and more, for Ywain told her some deal, and other deal she divined of herself. And when she had considered a little she bade him make haste and do those things for which he came, and look not to be long unharassed of his enemies: for that they had fastened an ill quarrel upon him by no chance but by intent, and they were such as would follow their craft.

So he went about the town busily, seeking
out all those which were friends to Hubert
and all those which were haters of evil
custom : and he found some and persuaded
other, and thought to have made good way.
And this time also he perceived how he was
favoured of the commons of Paladore; for
he discoursed to them hotly, and they were
ever assotted on discourse and on a burning
tongue.

And on a day he came down to the door
of his house, to go forth into the city : and
there came to his ears a sound of a bell
tolling and of a multitude of people going
all one way. And he hastened and came to
the end of the street and found them passing by; for they were going toward the
market-place. And he perceived that in the
middle was a train of some sort, walking by
two and by two, and there went a great bell
before them, and beside them the multitude
ran and jostled under the walls of the street.
And Ywain joined himself to them, for he

was willing to know of their dealing: and
for the thickness of the crowd he could not
see what was to the forward, but only he
perceived that in the train were many great
ones of the company of the Tower.

Then he spoke to a man that was beside
him in the crowd, and he asked of him
what might be the meaning of the concourse
and of the tolling: for the bell was of a
right dolorous sound, but among the people
was no sadness at all. And the man answered him: Well may you ask, as I also
have asked but a moment since, for the like
of this hath not happed within my memory.
And the concourse is all to see and to hear
the Archbishop a-cursing, and the bell also
is part of the cursing, for it betokens that he
which is cursed should be as it were buried
out of sight and fellowship. Then Ywain
remembered Hubert, and his heart rose and
he asked again: Whom then will they curse
and for what cause? And the man answered:
He is one Ywain, and I know him well: and

the cause is a true cause, for he is a blasphemer of the faith, a dealer in dreamage and all manner of sorceries.

And at that saying Ywain was astonished and said no more: for he had thought to hear speak of Hubert and not of himself. And he went forward strongly through the press, and came out into the market - place and stood upon a step under an archway and looked forth over the heads of the multitude. And he saw the train there before him: and in the forefront were an hundred of the company of the Tower, wearing their livery of black with a golden tower thereon. And after them came an hundred of clergy, apparelled in black clothes and white, and an hundred doctors of the schools with gowns of divers colours: and the Archbishop was robed in a silken robe of crimson with a great hat of the same, and before him went two with candles in hand, and one with a bell.

So they came upon the place in seemly

order, and they halted there and departed
into two lines the one over against the
other: and the Archbishop passed through
and stood upon the steps of the Great Hall.
And he held up his hand, and immediately
the bell ceased from tolling, and they of the
multitude were hushed from their babble.
Then came seven clergy before the Archbishop, having seven great candles in their
hands, and they stood and set light to them
and held them aloft: and when all the
people had perceived their dealing, then
they threw down the candles upon the
ground and trod out the flame of them.
And as they trod them they cried against
them: Out, out, accursed; until all were
quenched.

Then the Archbishop stood forth with staff
in hand, and he bade all men to know, and
to make known, how that Ywain was thence-
forth cut off from the company of all men
living, and from the company of all the
faithful dead. And under pain of the like

sentence he ordained that none should give him neither shelter nor speech, nor food nor fellowship, nor any means of life nor burial after death. And when he had so said he went solemnly out from the place: and all his train followed after him, and last of all went he that had the bell, a‑tolling dolorously.

CHAPTER L.

HOW YWAIN AND AITHNE CAME TO ALADORE
THE LAST TIME, AS IN THIS TRANSITORY
LIFE.

Now Ywain was known of none, for he was
in a sure place and looked forth above the
heads of the multitude. But he perceived
all that was done, and none better, and he
understood right well the evil malice and craft
of his enemies, and his heart was pricked
therewith as with the poison of wasps. And
the tolling of the bell he regarded not, neither
the treading of the candles, for he held such
things to be shows to frighten fools: but the
curses and the sentences, and all the words of
the Archbishop, those stung his blood and
made bitterness in his throat.

Then he thought to get some comfort of the people which were round about him, and he went forward a little and mingled with them and heard their talk. And at the first he had some pleasure of them, for there was not one in twenty but was making merry, with no saving of reverence, no, not of the Archbishop himself. But therewith came displeasure, that he also was but lightly accounted of: for the most part of the crowd made no distinction, but they cheapened the sin with the punishment. And the best that he could find was this, that the young and lean men were for him and the old and fat against him: for in Paladore the old dream not, save it be of gold and gluttony. And with this he was but ill content, for they which are young in that city are no more than one in three, and they are of small account, seeing that the best of them are banished.

So he left that and came away covertly to his own house, and he found Aithne therein, and told her of all that he had seen and heard.

And of the pain which he had in his heart, of
this he told her not, but she perceived it by
the manner of his speaking, for she knew his
thought as it were by touch and not by words.
And she said to him: It is no marvel if you
are in pain: for there is no venom in nature
like to the venom of speech, and many times
it will work madness in the blood. But there
is good magic against it, as I shall show you
presently, for this is a woman's gift from the
time out of mind. And bethink you also
how their curses are no better than their
ceremonies, and both alike folly: for they
are but tokens and have in them no power
to make good.

Nay, said Ywain, but they have this power,
that they hurt where they are aimed: for in
another man's case I had never regarded
them, but when they struck my own name
then they pierced and rankled. And thereat
he cast down his eyes and fell into a weariness.
And Aithne came to him and stood beside
him where he sat, and she took his head

between her arms and drew it in upon her
breast. And immediately the bands of his
weariness were loosed, and his spirit was
rocked in a sure hold as a young child is
rocked by his mother: and he shut to his
eyes and remembered no more the things
which were done against his peace.

Then he opened his eyes again, and he
saw how that he stood in a meadow of
flowers, and the flowers were kingcups and
lady-smocks and other such as are chiefly
loved of children. And among the flowers
there ran a little brook, and in the brook
were minnows going all one way like boats
upon a wind; and it seemed to Ywain that
it were worth all other joys if he might take
but one minnow in his naked hand. And not
far off from him stood a little maid and called
to him: and she called him to come home,
for it was time. And he knew that she was
his sister, that was his elder by two years,
and it was in his mind to obey her, but not
yet. Then he stretched out his hand and

stooped forward above the brook, and he
snatched suddenly at a minnow that was
there : and the sedge yielded beneath him
and he fell with his arms upon the water.
And immediately he came to his feet again
and stood upon the meadow: but he was
all bedabbled and bedrenched, and he feared
to be chidden, and his fear burst forth from
him and he wept.

Then the maid that was his sister came to
him and stood beside him, and took his head
between her arms and drew it in upon her
breast. And he shut to his eyes and immediately his fear was stayed and the water was
dried upon his arms and upon his feet, and
his heart was comforted. And he opened his
eyes again and looked about him, and he saw
the place wherein he was: and the place was
changed and was become Aladore, and he sat
by the margent of the sea, where he had been
aforetime, and Aithne was there beside him to
his solace.

And he said to her: O my beloved, what

enchantment is this that you have used?
For I have been a child again, and in great
grief concerning little things: and I have
been comforted with the comfort of my
mother and of my sister which are long since
dead and gone from me.

And Aithne stooped over him and kissed
him and said: Even so, beloved, and this
enchantment is no marvel, seeing that it is
common with them which are lovers of men:
for it is the gift of a woman, and an heritage
from the time that is out of mind.

CHAPTER LI.

OF TWO CITIES THAT WERE BUILDED DIVERSELY, AND HOW YWAIN AND AITHNE HEARD A HORN BLOWN OVER-SEA FOR BATTLE.

THEN said Ywain: Doubtless your saying is true, and well have I proved the gift: yet I marvel notwithstanding, for a man may wonder in despite of knowledge. And there is one matter concerning which I am still perplexed. And Aithne said to him: Say on. And he said to her: I am perplexed between two verities: for there is one truth of Paladore and another of Aladore, and though they be diverse yet they both have by seeming the nature of truth veritable. And many times my mind is in doubt concerning them: for

319

in our life that now is we come and go between two realms, and I would that I might know which of them shall outdure other.

And Aithne asked him : After what manner seem these verities to you ? And he answered : O beloved, now am I with you in Aladore, and all things else and all men and all places are but as shadows cast by this our life, and we move them as we will, and as we will we take away their being. But when I am alone and dwelling yonder among men, then have those shadows truth of substance and of touch, and the life of Aladore becomes an image in the mind, as it was aforetime when I saw it as a cloud in heaven.

Then Aithne was silent a space, and fear came into her eyes : and afterwards she spoke suddenly and said : O my beloved, keep innocency, for to a child these things are plain. And you were a child this moment past, and I with you : and wherefore now should we cloud our wisdom with a doubt ? And she rose up and said to him: Let us play a game together, as children that play upon the shore. For here is sand enough, and loneliness, and the tide returning: and we will build us two cities, and see which of the two shall best endure. And you shall build your city with your hands, and name it Paladore: and you shall make it in all things like to the city that you know, with a High Steep seaward, and a wall, and a gateway and towers thereon. And I also will make a city and name it Aladore, and I will make it after the same fashion, but not of the same substance: for I will not build it with hands but with a power of the spirit.

So Ywain took of the wet sand and of the dry, and he built him a great mound after the manner of children. And when he had made it strong then he carved it into the likeness of a city, with a high steep and a wall and towers thereon: and it stood upon the shore and looked out seaward, and he named it Paladore, for it was fashioned in no other wise, and the tide came running toward the edges of the steep.

Then Ywain said to Aithne: This is my city, O my playfellow, and I marvel that yours is not yet a-building. But Aithne answered him not, for she was singing a song of witchery: and she sang in a low voice and sweet, and as she sang she weaved a witch-knot upon the air with both her hands. And immediately there came a little mist upon the shore, and the mist drew upward from the sand and hung in one place upon the air like smoke: and so it continued the while Aithne sang her song. And when she had ceased from her singing then Ywain saw the mist no more, for it was clean vanished and in the place thereof was another mound and another city, in semblance like unto the first, and those two cities were nigh together upon the shore and the tide came about them both by little and little.

And Ywain and Aithne stood still and looked upon the tide: and it came running and lap-

ping more fiercely, and the froth of it began
to foam upon the edges of the mounds. And
the water gnawed upon the sand of the one
city, and that was Ywain's: and the walls
and towers of it began to crumble and to
crack, and at the last they were perished
wholly as by ruin of time, and the tide flowed
over them and they were gone. But with
Aithne's city it was not so, for the sea bit
not upon it nor overflowed it, but it stood
above the water until the turning of the tide.
And Ywain came near to touch it, but he
could not, for it was but mist between his
fingers. And he left it alone and stood and
looked upon it again: and it endured as rock,
notwithstanding it was builded of a song.

Then he said to Aithne: The game is
nought, for you have played it by no fair
hazard but by enchantment. And she answered him: Not so, for by this same enchantment is Aladore upbuilded and sustained,
and that is the truth of it. And she looked
into his eyes and her spirit entered into him,

and they twain were one spirit. And the
dusk began to fall about them and peace
therewith, for they were in their own place
beyond time and tide. But in that moment
came change upon Ywain, for a sound was
in his ears: and the sound was the sound of
a horn blown over sea, and in the hearing
of it all the blood of his body leapt furiously
up to battle.

CHAPTER LII.

OF A SHIP THAT WAS FULL OF LADIES AND LOVELY KNIGHTS, AND HOW YWAIN AND AITHNE DEPARTED WITH THEM OVER SEA.

THEN Ywain looked upon Aithne, and in one moment he remembered all her love and her kindness, and pain was mingled with his joy. And his heart was filled with a tumult past bearing, and he groaned aloud and cried: Ah! my beloved, what is this that has come upon us? For here is the land of our desire and the land of all loveliness and all delectable enchantments, and herein we might have had life enduring. But now I see well that there is no such fortune: for the horn has sounded, and the sound of it has power upon body and blood. And peace is gone from me suddenly, and I can by no means keep me from the

fight: for the cause is a right cause and one
that must be ransomed, yea, though all else
be given and lost for it.

But Aithne regarded him out of the depth
of her eyes, and she said: Grieve not, dear
heart, for how shall that which is given be
lost? And as for the life which dureth, that
is of the spirit and not of the body: for
consider them which were great lovers of
old time, how that they all are perished, as
in the world transitory, yet their souls dwell
not in death nor forgetfulness.

And when he heard those words Ywain's
heart was made strong again and his eyes
were lightened; and he saw his life as it were
a tale that shall be told. And he turned him
about suddenly, for he was aware how there
came somewhat from the seaward. And that
which came was a ship, going slowly under
stress of oars: and Ywain perceived that the
ship was builded after the fashion of old time,
and her sails were furled upon the yards, and
she came by her oarage landward against

the wind. And upon her deck stood many goodly persons: and they were all in silk or else in armour richly beseen, and they bore them gently and with a joyful courage.

Then Ywain was astonished, and he asked of Aithne: Who be these? for I know them not: yet their faces are like faces out of childhood. And Aithne answered him: You say not amiss, for these are they which are known of all men, howbeit none hath seen them, that is now on live. For yonder by the prow is Helen, fairest of women, and Paris, by whom Troy fell: and there is great Achilles that was loved both of maid and of man, and Prince Troilus that had double sorrow in loving of Criseyde, and Duke Jason that won the Fleece Perilous, and Medea that for his sake forsook her father's house. And hard by them is Sigurd of the Volsungs, and Brynhild the Queen, for whom he rode the Wavering Fire: notwithstanding they came never together, but they were proud lovers until death. And other two queens there are beside Brynhild, and they are Isoud and Guinevere; and with Isoud haunteth Sir Tristram, which drank with her the cup of sorrow, and with the lady Guinevere is that Sir Lancelot, that was never matched of earthly knight's hand.

Then Ywain looked, and he saw all those which were named, and other beside: and his heart was stirred with the sadness and the glory of them, and he asked again of Aithne: Tell me yet more of these lovers and of their renown, for of their loveliness is no need to tell. And Aithne spoke again, and she showed him where there stood a lady with a face like a flame of beauty, shining marvellously. And she said: Behold then Deirdre, that was born to be a death to many and a tale of wonder for ever. And with her is Naoise, son of Usnach, that loved her greatly. For when he saw her the first time, there and then he gave her the love that he never gave to living thing, to vision, or to creature, but to herself alone.

Notwithstanding she has a little grave apart.
And there also is Niamh, that Cuchulain
loved, and with three kisses she sent him to
his death. And there is Ailinn, daughter of
Lugaidh, and Baile of the Honey Mouth, that
died each for other, upon false tidings of
their death. And there is Nicolette the slave
girl, that was by rights the daughter of a
king, and had twelve princes to her brothers.
And beside her is her lord, that was her
lover through all, and Aucassin he was
called, and Count of Beaucaire thereafter.
And they four which haunt apart, by two
and by two together, they are Leila and
Majnun, whose love is the song of Araby
and the mirror of the East, and they are
Valeh and Hadijeh, that were parted by
land and by sea, yet at the last they came
together by the secret road of dreams.

So Aithne made an end of her telling, and
Ywain moved not but continued looking
upon the ship and upon them that were
therein. And his heart rejoiced in those

mighty dead and in the grandeur of the dooms that he had heard told of them. And the ship came onward and was driven of the oarsmen upon the beach, and they called to Ywain and Aithne that they should come aboard. So they took hands together and went aboard, and they were received joyfully of all those knights and ladies. And the ship was thrust strongly out from off the beach, and so turned seaward, and the sails were hoised upon the masts, and the wind filled them roundly, and all they that were aboard began to sing.

And Ywain knew not the song which they sang, but he perceived that it was a song of the Rhymer's making, for when he heard it he was mightily comforted, and he felt the springs of life leaping up within him. And the ship drave onward over foam and furrow and came swiftly upon a coast that was no strange coast: for upon it was the High Steep of Paladore, and the horn was blown again from the topmost of the city.

And by seeming that sound was well known
of the lovers that were in the ship, for when
they heard it they smiled and looked kindly
one upon another, as remembering old sorrow
long since lightened. And they brought
Ywain and Aithne to land, and kissed them
and bade them be of good courage, and so
to meet with them again, for they said how
their fellowship was an ever-during fellowship,
and might never be broken. Then the ship
put off from shore and went slowly to the
westward; and it was no more seen, for it
became as it had been a wreath of mist upon
the water. And Ywain and Aithne climbed
the steep together, and came into the city:
and the dusk was falling round them, and a
great star stood over Paladore.

CHAPTER LIII.

HOW YWAIN AND AITHNE CAME TO PALADORE THE LAST TIME, AND HOW THE SNOW FELL ALL NIGHT LONG.

THEN they looked upon that star, and as they looked they marvelled and were dismayed, for a great cloud came up and took the star from them utterly. And with the cloud came a wind, exceeding cold and bitter, and they perceived how that in one hour the year was turned to winter; and the wind got hold upon their bones and shrunk them, and their hearts were sick with silence and foreboding. Then the wind fell again suddenly, and the snow began to come thickly down the air, and it came upon their faces now driving and now feathering, in manner as the wind was still or gusty.

So they bent down their heads and went
through the city at speed, devising whither
they should go and of whom they should seek
counsel. And as they went they met one
which passed them by: yet by seeming he
knew them as he passed, and he stayed and
turned him about upon the street. And he
called not to them, but he made haste and
followed after them, and when he was come
near he looked about him warily and came
nearer yet. And Ywain peered at him through
the darkness and the snow falling, and he perceived that he was Dennis that had been
friend and fellow to him: and for all the pains
and curses that were against him Ywain misdoubted not of his faith. And as he trusted,
so it was: for Dennis took him and pressed
his hand, and he pressed it strongly in token
of friendship, but he spoke no word. Then
Ywain thought on danger and remembered
him of his enemies, and he bade Dennis go
before, in manner of one that had no knowledge of any beside himself, and so bring

them to some place where they might speak together. And Dennis went quickly before, and brought them into Aithne's own house, that was long time deserted and out of mind of all men. And when they were come there they entered in full silently, for they spoke no word, and their feet were dumb with snow. And they climbed the stairs groping, and came into the upper chamber, that was Aithne's, and made fast the door: and they darkened the window and kindled a little fire upon the hearth. And the fire took hold and grew, and they had joy of it, for in a fire there will be comfort against misery, as in a thing that hath life and fellowship.

Then they began to speak together, and Ywain asked of Dennis what should be the meaning of the horn which he had heard blowing. And thereat Dennis was astonished, as one that understands not what is asked of him: and at the last he said to Ywain: Whence are you come hither, and by what error deceived? For there has no horn been

blown in Paladore this year. Then he said
again: It is a marvel: for the blowing of
the horn is for to-morrow, and it is agreed
among us that at the sound of it the Eagles
shall draw together and make war against
them of the Tower.

Then said Ywain: So be it, and good end
thereto: yet without doubt I heard the horn,
and for that sake only did I come hither.
And Aithne said: I also heard it, and no
marvel: for there is a hearing of the spirit,
and many times one friend may perceive
another's counsel, and as well far as near,
and as well before as after.

And to that Dennis gave assent, for he had
heard the same of certain others: and he told
Ywain and Aithne of the counsel of the
Eagles. For their purpose was to bring in
Hubert and all other banished men, and they
would have no more such banishing henceforth, but all to live and let live. And they
devised to go upon their enemies by two ways
and so come against them unaware: and

namely that one party should take the gate
and the other party the great Hall. For
that Hall was the chief place of the city,
where was ever the concourse and the
government: and there should be their
stronghold and the blowing of the horn.
And at the sound of the horn should come
Hubert and his before the gate, and so to
break in with force. And though their emprise was hazardous, yet they looked to
achieve it, seeing that the Prince of Paladore
was suddenly departed out of this life without
survivors to inherit him, and by likelihood
the great ones would be in confusion.

So all these counsels Dennis showed unto
Ywain and Aithne, and it was long before he
made an end of speaking. And when he had
made an end they three sat silent, looking upon
the fire; and the logs crumbled upon the
hearth and the fire began to fail. And Ywain
rose up and unbarred the window to behold
the night: and the snow fell without ceasing,
and it lay in a great crust upon the sill. Then

Ywain sighed and shut to the window, for he was a-weary of the darkness, and he took wood and kindled the fire again, blowing upon the ashes with his breath. And they three outwore the night together, speaking of old things and things to come, and watching for the dawn.

CHAPTER LIV.

HOW THE HORN WAS GIVEN INTO YWAIN'S HAND, AND HOW HE SOUNDED THEREON A MORT ROYAL.

AND when it began to lighten towards dawn, then they went forth out of the house and made to go by the way of the market-place. And the snow had ceased from falling and it lay upon the ground before them deep and white, for it was yet untrodden. So they drew their cloaks about their faces and went quickly, to the intent that they should be known of none: and at the first there was no living soul that met with them. But afterward they had sight of three or four which came towards them, and by seeming they were the servants of some great one, accompanying with their master homeward.

And Ywain saw the lord of those men
coming behind them, and he knew him well,
for all that he was enwrapped against the cold.
And they drew near to pass by one another,
for there was no avoidance: and the lord
gave Ywain greeting and would have stayed
him, but Ywain muttered somewhat and so
passed on, and Aithne and Dennis with him.
And in truth this was Sir Rainald, that was
ever busy against other, and more especially
against the Eagles: and when he saw Ywain,
though he saw not his face, yet he misdoubted
him who he was. And Ywain looked after
him as he went, and he saw how he stood
staring upon the footprints in the snow: and
when he had considered them he followed
them backwardly, that he might find the house
from whence they had set forth.

Then Ywain turned him to Dennis, and he
said: What now? for we must make short
work. And Dennis stayed not, but ran quickly
towards the great Hall, and Ywain and Aithne
followed after him. And with a key Dennis
opened the door of the Hall, and they three

entered in : and there was no man within, but upon the wall was a great horn hanging, and Dennis took down the horn from the wall and gave it into Ywain's hand.

But Ywain said : How shall I blow for war that know but the hunter's notes ? For belike you have another manner for war, or else you are agreed among yourselves.

And Dennis answered him : Not so, but the sounding of the horn is enough, and no matter the music. For this is an ancient horn and a magical, and there is none among us that is able to sound it, save Hubert only : but it may be that you also are able, for there was a power upon you from the beginning.

Then Ywain went forth and stood before the door, and looked out over the city, and he saw it as a town of faery, for it was new and soft with snow. And he set the horn to his mouth, and blew therein with all his strength, and the note that he sounded was a mort royal : for he said within himself : God willing, we have hunted an evil thing to death.

And the sound of the horn blared out and went wide upon the air, and it came loudly into all the quarters of the city and into every street and every house, and there was no man in Paladore that heard it not. And they which heard it were awoke out of sleep, and the most of them groaned and turned them to their sleep again: but upon others came fear and hatred, and they got them quickly to their armour. And the Eagles also heard it and were glad, and they did on their swords which they kept in hiding, and issued forth to go upon their enemies.

But Ywain stood upon the head of the steps that were before the Hall, and he looked out over the city and saw no man stirring, nor he heard no sound of feet. And fear came upon him and loneliness and he thought upon Aithne and said to her: O my beloved, I have brought you to your death. And she answered him proudly: Nay, not yet: for you have sounded but once, and there are many faithful.

Then Ywain took the horn and blew it the

second time; and all they which were his began to run towards the place where he was, and they ran quickly, as men that thought not on danger, for joy that the time was come. And Ywain saw them how they came running, and his heart was uplifted with their joy and their fellowship, and his blood within him became like wine. And he set the horn to his mouth and blew it yet a third time, louder than before, and the sound of it smote the walls of Paladore, and the gates and the towers and the houses great and little, and all the whole city rang therewith, and the air trembled and the sky was filled with echoes.

Then the desire of battle came upon the Eagles and they ran together to Ywain and thronged upon the steps before him : and they lifted up their swords and shouted as it were one man, and the noise of their shouting went up mightily and was mingled with the echoes of the horn.

CHAPTER LV.

HOW THE EAGLES FARED IN FIGHTING, AND HOW SIR RAINALD WOULD HAVE DEALT WITH YWAIN.

THEN when the sound of the horn had ceased Ywain held up his hand and stayed the noise of the shouting, and he spoke and said to the Eagles how they should go with him to take the gate of the city, and so to bring Hubert in. And they all assented thereto and made them ready. But Ywain turned him about and looked upon Aithne, and a sharp pain went through his heart and he said to her: I am distressed, O my beloved, because of you: for to-day by the space of an hour we must be parted one from other. And I know not how to leave you, for I fear the great

343

ones of Paladore. And Aithne answered him lightly, and she said: Go now, and have no fear: for there is a chapel beside this Hall, and it is long time forsaken and forgotten, and there shall I be in sanctuary, until you come again. Then Ywain looked sadly at her, and she said to him: And if so be that you come not again, then in some other place shall you and I be met together. And she took him by the hand and led him in, and he went throughout the Hall and found the chapel as she had said: and they came by a bailey from the Hall into the chapel, and there they kissed and parted in the best manner that might be, as of lovers parting in dread.

Then Ywain came forth again to the Eagles, and he took a sword naked in his hand and went before them: and they came swiftly to the gate and looked to find it open, for they were agreed with the porter and with the guard. But they found it right otherwise, for the porter lay there slain upon the snow, and before the gatehouse was no guard, but a great company of spears. And Ywain perceived the malice of his enemy and he cried out to Dennis: This is that Sir Rainald, and he has outrun us by his craft, for I saw him running counter upon our trail.

And right as he was speaking there came a noise from without the gate, and Ywain and his shouted together and called on Hubert by his name. And they which were without heard them shouting, and they cried the war-cry of the Eagles, and battered with axes upon the gate. And Ywain called his company to rescue, and he went before them and they set on fiercely upon the spears, and the men of the Eagles and the men of the Tower hewed and thrust on this side and on that and were mingled furiously in battle. And for the space of half-an-hour they had no mastery either of other, but they swung back and forward like two wrestlers, seeking their advantage in great grips together.

Then at the last their breath began to fail them, and they drew a little apart and stood looking one upon another. And they of the Tower perceived how the Eagles were minished, for they were fewer from the beginning, and though they had slain each his man, yet were many of them dead upon the spears. And when the spearmen saw that they called each to other to go forward and make an end, and they came thrusting heavily upon Ywain and his, and by their weight they drove them backward. And more especially they thrust upon them by the right hand and by the left, that they might close them in on every side : but they prevailed not, for the street was narrow. Notwithstanding they continued thrusting, and Ywain perceived their intent, and feared it, for he saw how it should be when they were come into the market-place. And he gathered his strength together and shouted loudly to the Eagles; and they strove as men desperate, and lopped their enemies both spear and spearman, and so stayed them from their thrusting. Then when Ywain saw that they were stayed, he commanded the Eagles to be gone suddenly: and they ran back and escaped over the market-place, and came to the Great Hall and were gathered together upon the steps before the door.

And Ywain looked down from the steps and saw his enemies before him, and they were strong men armed and armoured, and they came running to the foot of the steps like the sea-tide upon the beach. And he looked back upon his own men and saw them few and faint, and it came into his mind that the end was not far off from them.

Then the spearmen made them ready again for battle, for they were strictly commanded that they should assault the place and stint not till they had taken it. So they came upon the steps with spears all thick together, as it had been thorns in a quickset hedge, and they began to push the Eagles upward from step to step. And Ywain saw their dealing, and he perceived the vantage which they had thereby, and the danger: for they were clumped so close that they could not move, except it were to go forward all together. Then he ran and stooped quickly, and he loosened a great stone of the flags which were before the Hall, and he came forward again upon the steps and cast it down upon the spearmen : and it fell like death among them, and they cried out piteously and went backward, and in their fear they trampled one upon another. And Ywain and his made haste and took up other like stones, for there was there no lack, and they stood ready to hurtle them down after the same manner : but the spearmen gave ground and would not abide their coming. And some among them clamoured that they should send for archers, to shoot safely upon the Eagles : and when the Eagles heard them clamouring they bade them good speed, for they knew how the archers were a free company, and favoured not the Tower. So the battle stood still on this side and on that, until that some new thing should fortune.

Then with watching the day began to pass

over, and the great bell of Paladore rang noon
above them. And in the same moment there
was a stir among the spearmen and the
throng of them was parted in the midst and
one came forth and began to go upon the
steps. And Ywain was astonished, for he
which came was Sir Rainald, and he came
courteously and without fear. And he gave
Ywain greeting, and looked cheerily therewith; and he demanded to speak with him
privily, and truce to be had between them
while they continued one with the other.

So they went into the Great Hall, they two
alone, and the door was shut to behind them.
And Sir Rainald began to speak with Ywain
as one that found no fault in him, but he
blamed only the Archbishop and his, and he
named their curses witless and unlawful.
And Ywain answered him: All this I have
forgotten, for I only am accursed: but to-day
our fighting is against a more evil custom,
and there is nothing shall stay us except
death only. Then Sir Rainald looked kindly
upon him and said: A pity of your fighting,

and of your friends: for there are few of them which are not slain or hurt. And the pity is this, that if you would, the weak should be the stronger.

Now when he had said these words he looked fixedly upon Ywain, and he took his hand and set a great ring upon his finger: and Ywain saw the stone of the ring, and in it were the arms of Paladore engraven. And Sir Rainald said: The Prince hath left none to inherit him, save you only: for there is none other that hath power in Paladore.

Then Ywain's heart fluttered like a bird in his bosom, and for a moment he thought to have escaped the death. Then his eyes were lightened and he remembered him of the Prince, how he had seen him in his chains. And he said to Sir Rainald: Take the ring again: for your princes have no power against your customs, else had they never been so bound. Then Sir Rainald took the ring and went out: and he spoke no word, nor he let no sign be seen upon his face.

CHAPTER LVI.

HOW YWAIN BEHELD A DEAD MAN LAID
ON BIER.

Now when Sir Rainald was departed the men
of the Tower made no more show of fighting,
but they drew off a little space and set a
watch upon the Eagles: and they fetched
wood and kindled them a fire, for the day
began to darken and the snow was cold about
their feet. And the Eagles kept their guard
upon the steps, for they durst not move therefrom, but their hope was that Hubert and his
should presently break in and rescue them.

And the dusk fell, and Ywain looked forth
over the market - place, and he saw a child
which walked alone and made to come from
the one side to the other openly. And by

351

his going Ywain knew him without doubt, and he was the boy by whom he had gone forth on pilgrimage. And he saw how the boy passed through the midst of the spearmen and they perceived him not: and though he trod downright upon the snow, yet he left behind him no footprint nor any mark of his going. And as he had passed through the spearmen so also he passed among the Eagles, and he came to Ywain and took him by the hand: and he led him through the Hall and through the bailey, and brought him to the chapel.

Now the chapel was dim with twilight, and Ywain entered within it and stood still; for he looked to see Aithne, and at the first he saw her not. But the child that was with him drew him by the hand, and he went farther, and came before the altar. And there upon the north side of the choir was a tomb beneath a canopy of carven stone, and the tomb was by seeming empty, for there was upon it no effigy, nor arms nor

words memorial; but beside it was Aithne in
sanctuary, and she was fallen asleep upon the
floor of the chapel. And Ywain regarded her
lovingly, and he had great comfort of her
beauty, seeing how she lay as one at rest
and upon her face was no care but only the
softness of sleep. Then the child left holding of Ywain's hand, and he went apart and
kneeled upon the step which was before the
altar, and there he folded his hands together
and bowed his head: and when Ywain saw
him so kneeling, then upon him also fell
peace and quietness of heart. And he bowed
his head after the like manner, and when he
lifted it up he saw the child no more.

Then he heard above him the sound of a
bell that was tolling stroke by stroke, and
the door of the chapel was opened behind
him and the sound of the bell came in clearly,
and with it came a wind as cold as death.
And Ywain turned and saw how there entered
in six men in white clothes and black, with
hoods about their faces: and they bore upon

their shoulders a bier, and that which lay thereon was covered with a pall. And the three which were on one side were all in black, and the three which were on the other side were all in white: and they set down the bier before the altar and kneeled beside it. And there came in after them a great company of knights, and they were all armed and visored, and their surcoats above their armour were of black or else of white. And with that company the chapel was fulfilled from end to end and from side to side, and in every knight's hand was a candle burning; and the flame of the candles was clear and bright, and wavered not for any wind.

Then one stood forth between the altar and the bier, and prayed aloud; and the words which he prayed were old words, yet was their sound stranger than an unknown tongue. And thereafter he began to sing a solemn chant, and all the company of knights made their response: and the sound of their chanting went over Ywain as it were the

deep sea closing up his eyes. And he strove
with all his force, whether to move from
that place or to cry out, for he was in an
agony: but neither his body moved nor his
tongue gave utterance.

Then he that said the office made a sign
of blessing, and the knights fell down upon
their knees. And afterwards they rose up
altogether and chanted again right joyfully,
and they went forth singing, and the sound
of their voices came back out of the night.
And they left there the bier before the altar,
and at the head of it were seven candles
burning.

Then Ywain was loosed from his bondage
and his spirit returned into his body, and he
wept silently because his agony was past.
And he longed to find the meaning of that
which he had seen, for in his life-days he
had seen many visions and dreamed many
dreams, but none like to this, neither for
dread nor for deliverance. And as he thought
thereon he cast his eyes upon the bier, and

when he beheld it he knew that the vision
was not yet ended, seeing that this also was
part of it.

Then he went forward, for his feet drew
him; yet he trembled also and his heart
was shaken, and he had great need of hardi-
hood. And he came trembling and stood
beside the bier and looked down upon the
pall: and under it was the semblance of one
lying alone. And Ywain put forth his hand
and took hold on the edge of the pall, and
he drew back the pall upon the bier and
looked and saw the face of him which lay
thereon. And when he beheld it, in that
same instant there came into his mind
remembrance of all deeds that ever he had
done, and he saw them afar off, and some
of them were as lights which flare up and
fade again, and other of them were as fires
which smoulder and will not be put out.
And in like manner he remembered all men
and all women whomsoever he had known,
and he saw them afar off and had pleasure

in them all: for he saw them not as doers of good and of evil but as pilgrims only, and every one walking by the light that was in him.

Then he stretched out his hand and took the pall again to cover the face of the dead. And when he had covered it he stood a long time questioning: for the face which he had seen was his own face, and it was secret as silence is secret.

CHAPTER LVII.

OF A BATTLE BY FIRE AND HOW YWAIN AND AITHNE WERE NO MORE SEEN IN PALADORE.

THEN Ywain heard a voice which called him by his name, and it was the voice of Aithne, and she came to him and stood beside him. And he said to her: Come not nigh the bier, for there is one thereon which hath a secret in his face. And she said: I also have seen that face, for I saw it in a dream. And for the secret, be not troubled overmuch, for the end is coming when all things shall be made plain. Then said Ywain: O beloved, I doubt not: but when I looked upon the dead I trembled, and I tremble yet, for the face will not be gone from me.

Then Aithne came near to him and stood before him, and she laid her hands upon his forehead and closed up his eyes. And immediately his care went from him, and he was covered round as with soft wings of peace. And afterwards Aithne drew down her hands from off his face, and he looked before him: and the bier was vanished and that which lay upon it, and the place was void. Howbeit the seven candles were not vanished, but they stood burning in seven great candlesticks, and the flames of them were like seven spearheads of gold.

So they two stood hand in hand and looked upon the light: and in the same instant there came a noise of shouting from before the Hall, and they ran hastily and came forth upon the steps. And there beneath them was the whole place filled with torches and with spears, and they heard their enemies shouting fiercely against them. And they heard also the sound of bowstrings, and the arrows came thick about them: and upon every arrow was a pennon of quick flame, and they came through the night like fiery serpents flying. And some of the arrows entered into the Great Hall and lit upon the beams and upon the carven wood: and the flame licked upon the wood, and there was no force to stay it. And Ywain saw well that the end was come, for there was no rescue, and the fire began to roar among the timbers of the roof: and in his heart was no more care, but he rejoiced with a new joy, such as he had not known in all his days. And he came forth before his people, and in his right hand he took his sword, and in his left hand he took the hand of his beloved. And he looked down upon the faces of his enemies and he laughed aloud and cried to them: Come near and take what is left of the night, for to-morrow is ours and all that is to come.

Then the arrows flew more thickly, and the torches came onward with the spears, and the place was filled with flame and death. And Ywain and Aithne went swiftly down, and all their people with them: and the battle swayed about them heavily, and they were no more seen.

CHAPTER LVIII.

OF A TOMB THAT WAS FOUND IN PALADORE, AND OF DIVERS SAYINGS THAT WERE HEARD CONCERNING IT.

IN the same hour came a noise of shouting from the West, and Hubert and his broke in upon the battle. And they struck upon the spearmen as the wood-knife strikes upon the ashlings, so that there was neither resistance nor recovery, but all laid to length upon the ground. And when they had made an end of their enemies, then they sought busily to find their fellows, if there might be any with the life yet in them. And they found of them one here and another there, for they were buried beneath the slain: but Ywain and Aithne they found not, neither sign of them, neither report.

And when it was morning light then they made search again: and they came into the chapel wherein Aithne had been in sanctuary. And there also they sought, and when they came before the altar and saw the tomb that was thereby, then they found that which they sought not. For upon the tomb were two lying in semblance of a man and a woman: but they were fashioned of black bronze after the manner of the tombs of kings. And the faces of them were the faces of Ywain and Aithne, and they lay there as they had been sleeping.

And they which saw them marvelled: and one said: They are here sleeping, and belike they will come again from their sleep. And another said: Nay, how shall this be; for they were but man and woman, like unto ourselves. But Hubert rebuked them both, for he said: They are not here but otherwhere, and their sleep is but a semblance.

Aladore

And doubtless the pilgrim hath achieved his pilgrimage, for he learned of his lady: and she came and went of her own magic, and had from her birth the Rhymer's heritage.

THE END.